THE
SPECTACLE
AT THE
TOWER

THE
SPECTACLE
AT THE
TOWER

——

GERT HOFMANN

TRANSLATED BY

CHRISTOPHER MIDDLETON

Fromm International Publishing Corporation

New York

Designed by Constance Fogler
Printed in the United States of America
First U.S. Edition

Library of Congress in Publication Data
Hofmann, Gert
The Spectacle at the Tower
I. Title
PT2668.0376A913   1984   833'.914   83-27472
ISBN 0-88064-013-8

THE
SPECTACLE
AT THE
TOWER

1

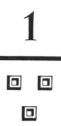

It was in the fall of last year, we were traveling through Sicily, tormenting each other to death again, in her old car, too, which, past Canicatti, would only move, no, crawl along in first gear, and eventually around noon, after leaving the autostrada to look for a repair shop—a mistake —and taking to vaguer and vaguer side roads that led deeper and deeper into the scorched and trackless interior, the *zona morta*, we came to a stop finally at the crumbling walls of D. And immediately on getting out, as I circled the car helplessly amid the drumming of the cicadas, I noticed—it was anything but an illusion—that the sweetish smell of carrion that lies over this whole island seemed to be sweeter here, stronger, even more repugnant. Right, so I get out. And have no idea that our fate is actually sealed by my doing so. Our separation, shortly thereafter—but only in appearance—canceled, is, so to speak, already accomplished, our tour of the place has begun, the tower seen, the corpse turned on its back. Horrified, we stoop over it, looking for the death-dealing wound. All of which, because I'm getting out of the car, even if we have no inkling of it, now lies in store for us. But all around me there's gorse, laurel, ferns, fleshy ferns that grow waist-high, and, because there has been no rain this year for eight months, have a thick film of road dust on them, snowlike, a horrible sight. And I recall that this fern is the oldest plant of this region, a makeshift and temporary covering for the remnants of a land bridge once joining Africa to Europe, but probably destroyed in the tertiary epoch. And the volcanic rock under my feet is the oldest stone that exists, dating back to a time when this earth consisted of nothing else. Forget it, I'm thinking to myself, and I glance up at the earth brown houses stooped toward me, through which a hot and oppressive wind is blowing. And even if I haven't seen it, I've detected, narrowing my eyes, the image of a wholly beautiful classical landscape. How happily one could live here! Here, looking out into this perfect landscape, this village called Dikaiarcheia, this small, ruined, dust-blanketed village, touched only here and there with subdued green, this poverty-stricken, horrible, and repulsive place. From the very start it seemed a bit weird to me. The name means City of the Just, too, imagine! How could people ever live here, I was asking myself, while Maria, my wife, whom I want finally to leave after seven years of marriage, stays shut in our car, her car, with windows rolled up and doors locked, on which I insisted, "even if you suffocate," I told her. And foremost in my mind, as I turn my back on her and with one stride enter the unknown village through a gap in the wall, I keep her tear-stained, desolate, pale face—what became of our holiday suntan this year?—behind the closed car window, carrying it carefully over the stones and through the ferns into the place called D. Because there is this situation: when she admitted to me this morning that she might be pregnant, I told her that I didn't want the child, because, besides herself and our Adriana, there was also an illegitimate child of mine, three years old, a boy, Mario, in L., about twenty kilometers away from where we live, "about whom you've known nothing and for whom I have to provide as well." She looked at me for a long time and didn't want to believe me. Briefly: it was only with the greatest difficulty that on this Wednesday afternoon I found in Dikaiarcheia a mechanic who would take the car into his garage and see what could be done and have it ready again, perhaps, by the morning, and then to find for my wife and myself, for one night, in the Hotel Lucia, a room, even if it had no bath, no shower, no running water. At ground level the window looked out over a dusty *piazza* with an immense African umbrella pine in it. I've seldom come across such stark poverty, misery, and filth as in Dikaiarcheia. And we dragged in our luggage, which for obvious reasons we couldn't leave in our car, soaked in sweat, not a soul to help us, for in D. we saw for a long time not a single person, except for a few ragged children playing with a goat in front of the hotel, because nobody was there, or because everyone had retreated from the heat into their houses, to peer at us, the foreigners, through cracks in doors and windows, to watch us unseen, to keep their eyes on us. Anyway: our luggage, and that meant her suitcases with dresses and skirts and all her toilet things, against which I had advised her and on which she had insisted—she wanted to go dancing!—and not one of which, during our trip, now in its third week, just as I'd foretold, she had unpacked or carried or used, all this we had to drag, going back and forth I don't know how many times, out of the broken-down car, up a steep unpaved pathway, through the gap in the wall, and into our hotel room, with its rickety door, a room of the utmost simplicity imaginable. And once again I realized: Too much, we have too many possessions. Anyway we've brought too much with us, I told myself, piling it all up in one corner. It was an even taller pile than I'd thought. And out of it, aware of the perils besetting our accumulated belongings, I took the most valuable things—my wrist-purse with the money, checks, and passports, also my two cameras, which I hung around my neck and from now on for the whole day and half the night, and, lengthwise, through the entire village of D., to the tower and up the tower, I simply carried them with me, on me. I'd never believed two cameras could be such a burden, so confining. And the room, which has only one window, with a wooden shutter, and so it's dark, dingy, and oppressive, was at one time certainly a stall for calves or goats, one can smell it. Its whitewashed walls have great blank stains, while its ceiling, from which the plaster is falling away, is so low that I can reach up and, without any effort, not even standing on tiptoe, touch it with my fingertips. Naturally such a covering is oppressive to a person like me, sensitive and easily upset, even if I'm tall and heavy—a person who needs plenty of space, upward too, it hangs heavily over the head, so that as soon as I'm in the room there's an obstruction. Briefly, the room we've been given turns out to be an insult to us, who are guests here, but probably it's the only room in the place. For it's obvious that at this time of the year, in the off-season, no, at all times, guests or foreigners would never, or only most infrequently, end up in this place. People here don't know what a guest is. And aware of this ignorance and this infamy and oppressive overhanging weight and of the menace to my own thoughts and feelings and of our powerlessness and lostness —soon, too, I'll be involved in the most serious, most brutal argument of our whole married life—we dragged ourselves, because I'm hungry and thirsty, to the far end of the corridor into the equally gloomy and vacuous dining room, with only flies to enliven it, flies to *endeaden* it.

2

The dining room—where, after a meal of macaroni and a piece of tough, stringy meat cooked with many bay leaves and a lot of rosemary, I supposed it was rabbit, my wife had no opinion and ate none of it, either, also two or three pitchers of wine, no salad, no dessert, nothing, we stared at each other across the table, speechless and embittered, no, with loathing. A mistake, this whole journey, as we both now knew, though we weren't yet saying so. Rather, my wife, who has been crying incessantly since I broke the news to her, and who is supposedly unwell (!), now wanted me to tell her who was the mother of Mario, the boy I've seen only once in my life. It was then that I leaned back in my chair and began to explain things to her, in a few terse words, for there's nothing to be said about that woman. And while I was speaking, in short, clear, sober sentences, I suddenly noticed, to my horror, that outside, under the pine tree, the children weren't playing with the goat anymore. No, I saw, while slowly uttering the phrases that were so hurtful to my wife and fatal, probably, to our marriage, saw quite clearly—they've got a knife now, they're tormenting the goat, now they're killing it with the knife! Since I'm sitting so as to look through the window directly at the pine tree, whereas my wife has her back to the window and the tree—I can see every detail. Five of them, as at a signal, the children, all boys, all filthy, all in rags, all handsome, have suddenly flung themselves on the goat, they have, as I, with the cameras slung over my shoulders, can observe quite clearly from my hard chair, taken hold of the goat by its ears and legs and tail, and then a handsome slim boy, who incidentally had a red scar on his forehead, with great effort and with both hands has stuck a knife, which he brandished gleaming in the sunlight a few times, a long knife probably not sharpened for ages, into the throat, turning it: so as to enlarge the hole in the neck on all sides —he works rapidly—and gradually, first downward and then upward, to cut through the throat.

Don't turn round, Maria, I've exclaimed, something you'd better not see is happening behind you. And as was to be expected my wife has looked at once behind her and seeing immediately the blood that has dropped from the goat she has uttered a loud scream.

Now you know, I've said; all because you don't listen to me. And while the goat, which won't be dead for quite a while, goes on giving its death bleat, I've continued my account of my relations with Mario's mother, "about which you needn't bother in the least," I've said, or something similar, "for they've always been very casual and random, and she herself is a quite ordinary woman, though

9

perhaps attractive." And: I've said something coarse, the way one does, and shrugged my shoulders, and assured her that there's no point in shedding tears now—as I probably expressed it—"over such a mundane fact as a three-year-old child." For me, I exclaimed, my gaze fixed on the goat which has now sunk to its knees, this child doesn't exist, you've no need to trouble yourself about that, for me this child is dead. And then, while I'm beginning, despite, no, because of the unforeseen misery of our surroundings, which has stunned both of us, because of their comfortlessness too, and despite or because of the beastly thing done under the pine tree, as I'm beginning to tell her that I've decided, definitely now, and irrevocably, to leave her, if her pregnancy is not stopped at once, the door of our "dining room" opens, the last thing we'd expected, with a curious grinding sound, as of teeth, and in comes a man, forty, forty-five, fifty years old perhaps, small as all Sicilians are, but broad-shouldered and well-nourished, in a black suit, with white pinstripes, a Sunday suit, but crumpled, his robust body forced into a white shirt, which is much too tight and strangling for him, especially at the neck— the necktie!—in he comes, takes a look at us, and walks toward us. At once I startle, don't know why, at once I think no good will come of this, and wonder at once: What does he want? And at once, don't know why, think it's my wife's fault. And I say to her quietly: Look! and quickly pass to her under the table my handkerchief, to wipe her tears away with, but she is so full of bitterness and loathing that it's all the same to her, and she pushes the handkerchief back to me, and I put it away again.

And then the man is standing before us, at the table.
Tedesco, he asks, *o Inglese?*
Jaja, I say, and, because I want to get rid of him quickly,
I don't even look up, but watch how, outside, on the *piazza,*
the blood of the goat to the throb of its last heartbeats is
spilling from its now gaping neck and severed throat into
a yellow plastic pail that one of the children is holding
under it.

Deutsch! the man exclaims, and he grins and then even
rubs, I believe, his hands. Instead of speaking Italian to us
(or Sicilian), or at least trying it out, from the start he
speaks to us in German, very ably, very fluently, if not
always quite correctly, but by all means resourcefully.
For, like all Italians, he obviously takes pleasure in his
formulations, which I—not my wife!—shall soon share,
even if the inner rhythm of his thinking remains to the
end unintelligible to me. I still grasp the sense, even if not
that of every single phrase. And in this German, which
would be excellent if he'd only accentuate his words somewhat differently, he explains to us that he, as the local
supervisor, yes, that's what he calls himself, has been at
once informed of our arrival and has hurried over, glad
to be able to welcome us in Dikaiarcheia, at last, at last!
And with one of the powerfully exaggerated gestures
common in these areas, he spreads his arms, doesn't
embrace us, but simply rubs together his slack red hands.
At the same time his hair and skull are suddenly enveloped
in a swarm of flies, which, I swear, was not previously in
the room. And then the man, fanning away from his face
the flies that annoy even him, wants to know from us if

we came alone, or if we might be members, or possibly
the advance guard, of a larger tourist agency? While
saying "tourist agency" he glances around the dining room
a few times, hoping to discover, at other tables, other
"members," who might have eluded him, but the room,
as he sees, is empty except for ourselves. And here, finally,
I intervene and restrain him from elaborating any further
on whatever ideas he might have, shouting at him, with
an energetic wave of my hand: Alone! We're alone!
O well, even then, he says, not hiding his disappointment,
but . . . Yes, he shows it.
Listen, I say, since the whole thing is obviously based on
a misconception, because we are both, my wife and myself,
traveling as individuals, on our own initiative, and fundamentally solo, and, at this particular moment, very much
concerned with one another, if not contrarily so. Another
pregnancy, imagine! Or, I tell myself, this is the start of
one of the customary local gags, in which we, however, as
the dupes, will have no part, no, we refuse. But here, with
his swarm of flies clinging all around him, the supervisor
interrupts me. With a bow, which calls for the opening of
his black coat, revealing a heavy gold watch chain, a pair
of brightly embroidered old-fashioned suspenders, and a
broad strawberry red sash, which he has hastily looped
around his upper body, the badge of a particular Order,
perhaps, or the distinguishing mark of local supervisors,
or it merely shows his liking for color, or it could be
swank: Even if we haven't come with a group, he asks,
mightn't we have heard of a grand folkloristic spectacle

and have come, solo or not, to D. on that account? Or the
question differently put: What word of this spectacle—
perhaps he also says *my* spectacle—has been spread abroad,
in foreign parts, perhaps? And when he says "spectacle"
he licks, how horrible, his lips! My reply is brief and
truthful, for neither back at home nor anywhere else have
we heard about a folkloristic spectacle in D., we haven't
even heard of D., but I have only one thought in my
crushingly oppressed head, and that is to get rid of this
man and his swarm of flies as soon as possible, so as to have
put my crucial talk with my wife and thus my seven
married years behind me as soon as possible, *once and for
all*. And I'll be careful not to incur, considering the bill
for car repairs, which I don't like to contemplate, to be
paid very early next morning, any further financial lia-
bilities. And thirdly, because my extreme caution has
forbidden me to shed my cameras and wrist-purse, but I've
had them, even during the meal, slung around my shoulders and hanging from my wrist, I feel rather ridiculous.
With a purse on one's wrist, as anyone knows, how can
one eat? For which reason I'm afraid he might be laughing
at me secretly. So I exclaim, as curtly as possible: No, no,
no! and then I even stamp my feet beneath the table.
Well, then, he continues, more or less, in any case we've
come just at the right moment, as by a miracle—perhaps
he also said: as by an act of grace—for the aforementioned
unique spectacle, because it just happens that the spectacle
is set for this evening, at eight o'clock, thus—out of his
waistcoat pocket he extracts a large silver watch—about

five hours from now. And that he's at our disposition, to take us to it and explain everything. And that there'll be drinks and snacks, *gratis*, he says, *gratis*.

I'm thinking: Good God, doesn't he understand, or does he not want to understand? I'm thinking that this is the last straw, given our present situation: to have a witness between us, someone else around. How should I ever tell her of my decision, if there's someone else around? And anyway I'm thinking: I know your sort, supervisor, and I recall with disgust the clichés of those "guides" who are incapable, even face to face with the frescoes at Pompeii, of anything but enumerating the colors that anyone can see for himself. And after all: in a filthy hole like D., which God evidently abandoned long ago, what kind of a "spectacle" can there possibly be? Here we are, stuck in the boondocks. So, telling my wife with a look that we'll soon be rid of this man and that our talk, not that she'll like it, will soon continue, I show my astonishment at the supervisor's suggestion, I express displeasure, annoyance, impatience. No! I shout, the spectacle doesn't interest us, we don't need anyone to take us to it. And I hit the table, twice even, I believe, with the flat of my hand, or anyway I feel like hitting it, twice or three times, but then my attention is distracted again from outside. Where, beneath the pine tree, out of the miserable goat, which still can't believe what's happening is true, but is struggling and bleating from its throat, the last blood is running. Who'd have thought there could be so much blood in such a small animal.

Yes, yes, the supervisor exclaims.

14

What? I ask, looking outside.

Someone, he says, looking freely around, someone must accompany you.

Where? I ask.

Yes, yes, he exclaims. So that you can find the tower.

The tower? I ask.

Yes, the tower, he says, and he draws a huge, colored, probably hand-stitched handkerchief out of the pocket of his black trousers, which are much too tight, almost bursting, shiny as if polished. Someone, he says, and he wipes his forehead, who can explain everything to you.

How do you mean, *explain*? I say.

Because, he says, it's important. I mean the history of D. in general, and also that of the spectacle, but also all the background stories, which also exist, just as everyone knows there's a world behind the world. . . . In short: We needed him!

As for me, now that I'm gradually recovering from the surprise and ruckus of his entrance—he also walks with an impediment—and am now finally finding my way out of the conversation with my wife into the entirely different, equally unpleasant, already equally overprotracted situation, also because I've drunk some wine, even if it was cheap, sour, and bad, I now increasingly feel more than a match for this man, when I see his sweat-drenched shirt collar, his stubbly double chin, smell his stale breath. And then suddenly I see that he is quite brazenly—I can hardly comprehend it, my wife at once looks the other way—stroking his member inside his tight trousers, and moving it about, from right to left, I think. All right, it's him, not

15

me, who's the ridiculous figure, the buffoon, in this oppressive, low-ceilinged room. Of course he's ridiculous, I'm thinking, how can you have missed seeing it? Also I have the advantage of sitting, even if I'm heavily festooned, whereas he, although he's unencumbered, has to stand before me. And I've stretched my legs out and now I stretch my arms out, too, because, if need be, I mean to stop this man from approaching, uninvited, even closer to me and from perhaps taking hold of me, patting me, in the Mediterranean way. And I exclaim—thinking, look out, any moment now he'll kiss your hands—in order to nip in the bud any such, and *worse*, confidences between us: We're certainly delighted—and surprised—at his good German, which we certainly hadn't expected to find in this evidently untouristic and somewhat singular little world— I point toward the *piazza* . . .

Immediately he interrupts.

His good German, he says, is due to this: He has lived for a fairly long time in Germany, in Frankfurt, until, because of a misunderstanding, the authorities suddenly took him to the border and pushed him out, otherwise he'd not be here at all, not on any account.

Well, now, I say, and for a moment look at him sharply, where did you live then?

In Frankfurt, of course, he says.

And why, I ask, were you taken to the border and pushed out?

Mistaken identity, he says. And he starts, as an indication of his knowledge of Frankfurt, to enumerate several street

names, Moselstrasse and Elbestrasse, and then even a few
hotels, like the Hotel Eder.

Spendid, splendid, I exclaim, I see that you know Frankfurt.

Naturally Taunusstrasse, too, he says.

Yes, yes, I exclaim, you're a much-traveled man. But now,
as for attending a spectacle at the tower or a tour of the
village of D., I continue, of that, since we've already
visited Palermo, Syracuse, Agrigento, Messina, and Cefalù
—here I'm lying—and are fascinated by everything, the
whole island, there can be no question. We know everything here, I exclaim, we know just everything here! And
look, besides, I say, while one of the children is lightfootedly carrying the pail with the blood away—who
knows where—this journey my wife and I have been on
has been long enough, we're rather . . . And anyway, I
exclaim. Perhaps we've been on the road together too long,
I say, too often, and I try to look my wife in the eye, but
she's looking down, so that we're altogether apathetic, and
one another's presence, each by the other's presence . . .
Look at her, does she look like a woman on holiday with
the man she loves, I exclaim, and point to my tearful,
shattered, and harried wife. But then I realize that I
shouldn't have said this and have gone too far with my
confidences. No, I'm exaggerating, I exclaim, actually it's
quite the reverse. It's me who's exhausted, not her, I
exclaim, not her. So it's not her but me you must look at,
I exclaim, trying to make up for my tactlessness, it's me
who's under a strain, which is actually the case, as I see it.

First the annoyance at the pregnancy, which may be real,
then the car suddenly stops, then dragging the luggage
and the briefcases, and now sitting around, waiting. And
all of this in this heat and under this pressure from above,
whereas I want to get moving, but how? And I even give
myself a shake, I believe, at the thought of a tour of D.
The fact is that everything we've seen of D. so far gives us
cause enough to fear what we might come across. A little
goat, imagine that! Children, et cetera. Now, as I see,
spattered with blood, hands, knees, et cetera. But I say
nothing of this, only that we're sorry, but for various
reasons, which I won't specify, we'll dispense with a tour
of D. And to indicate that the conversation is at an end,
I pour, because nothing more conclusive occurs to me—I
should have stood up, I should have taken Maria, we
should have walked away—the last mouthful of wine from
the pitcher into my glass and, although I'm probably red
in the face as it is, drink it in one gulp. And then I place
the glass as decisively and firmly as possible on the table
before me. And wipe my mouth with my sleeves, first
right, then left. That's that. But the supervisor notices
none of this, back into his jacket he shoves the cuffs that
had slid out when he made his bow—unlike his gleaming
collar they're a little murky—and he says that Sicily is
large and has much to offer, from the most sublime to the
contrary, yet everything is worth seeing.
And what's the contrary, I exclaim.
What's more, he says, and he has a broad swath of light
across his face, the sights here in D. have been deliberately
brought together, precisely for people like you, who are

tired from seeing so much, in a very small space, so there's no question of your having to walk, crawl, climb, or anything so strenuous.

And what is there to see, I exclaim, and what is the contrary?

Unfortunately, the supervisor says, if you compare the place with others, especially those you've already been so good as to visit, places of which all of us are proud, even if we don't all live in those places and cannot have any share in their beauty—but in D., he suddenly exclaims, in a rather loud voice, somebody has to be living, and D., although it offers little at first glance, has to be seen!

And what, I exclaim, listen to my question now, what has it to offer? What is the contrary?

Because—and this is roughly his reply—alas, of our history and our myths, which do live on within us, to be sure, they certainly do, virtually no visible traces are left. Nothing one can show to a cultivated foreigner from far away, who is eager for beauty and history. Hardly any traces over which one would like to linger, he complains, presumably he means classical antiquity. A few blackened stones between their unfortunately rather *disinhabited* houses. A few reconstructed vestiges of walls in front of their tiny tile factory, long inactive because not in demand. Despite years of excavation, he exclaims, nothing, so that a person might easily consider sparing himself a journey to D. Yet: that's where he would have been mistaken.

You're referring to the contrary? I ask.

To what? he asks.

Just as I thought, I say.

So that finally, he continues more or less, we had set our hopes for a time on the catacombs, but the catacombs are another story. Personally, I'm convinced, he says, that D. is located on top of the largest network of catacombs in the world, but the conviction is one I cannot prove at the present time. And now the municipal authorities, so as to avoid accidents, have had all the entrances to all catacombs sealed up, so it's no longer possible to visit them. But the catacombs exist, you must believe me, even if I can't show you them. And suddenly he starts—isn't it ludicrous?—to stamp on the floor with his feet. Listen to them, he exclaims.

You mean? I say and sit up a little.

Well, the catacombs, of course, what else? he exclaims and points to the floor.

Certainly, I say, although I hear nothing at first, but then, as the stamping goes on, it really does sound for a moment as if the floor were hollow. And then as I sink back into my wicker chair, indeed this whole afternoon I'm restless, sit this way and that, shift around, would prefer to get up and go, I happen to glance through the window again, and I see that the goat, now done for, drained of its blood, the size of its body seemingly shrunk, lying there headless— the head lies beside it—with limp legs stretched out, on the ground, is being chopped into pieces by the children, who can't see me, however, with a kind of axe. With an axe? Yes. Even the supervisor glances at the pieces, but then he simply goes on talking, and regrets that they have nothing but the catacombs left. Therefore, he exclaims, the tower.

And that we absolutely must attend the spectacle which will be taking place around the tower.

You mean? I say and suddenly I'm sitting upright in my wicker chair.

Yes, I do insist, he says.

What? I ask.

Attend the spectacle, he exclaims, and stamps, attend it.

And before that you were saying? I exclaim.

Nothing's left, he says.

No, the other thing, I exclaim.

The other thing? he asks.

Yes, the thing you said in between, I say.

You mean the tower?

Yes, I exclaim, I mean the tower. And I'm thinking: Might there really be something after all? And that what there is, is a tower. And at the word *tower*, I don't know why, perhaps it's the simultaneous sight of a half-naked boy, also—but I've already said it—he's very handsome, very dark, only slightly spattered with blood, I'm perhaps a little aroused. Might the excitement about the boys have— something to do with excitement about the tower? For when the tower was first mentioned I wasn't yet aroused, but I'd managed to accept the tower, and the boys too, as something quite natural and ordinary. But now there's a difference. Suddenly the idea of the tower arouses me.

So now I'm asking where it is.

This way, the supervisor says and points the way out through the door.

Far? I ask.

No, he says.

High, I ask.

Yes, he says.

And if one may ask, what sort of a tower is it, I ask.

Just a tower, he says.

Just a tower?

Yes, he says, and he scrapes his boot soles on the floor, just a tower.

A tower, I say, and I'm thinking: So there's a tower! And I draw a deep breath and feel how all of a sudden from the idea of a tower a great but vague fascination, a powerful but indefinite expectation comes over me from the mere utterance by me—far too loud, finally even shouted —of the word. So there's a tower, a tower! And this tower, which we'll soon see and eventually climb—only we don't yet know this—is what we are and should be talking about. Although at this point the word suggested nothing clear and definite to me, but, rather, an evasively fluttering and fragmentary notion of something tall, strong, firm, around which one walks, looking upward, this afternoon, in this dining room *endeadened* by flies and *other things,* at the wooden table which is rough as a file, with my wrist-purse hard between my legs, I've been thinking of this tower for a long time now. What's the meaning of this? For since, as we all know, no man really thinks, it's just now and then that notions occur to him (or not) and he calls these notions thoughts, which he arranges in a sequence— in any case I've been arranging my few notions about the word *tower,* without reaching any conclusion, quite the contrary. Yet also, in all the regional guidebooks that are known to me, and there are many on the market, some in color, some in black and white, some with illustrations, some without, there's no mention of a tower. But then in the guidebooks there's no mention of D., either. Well, now, a tower in D!

The *Torre di Dikaiarcheia!* exclaims the supervisor, boastful, raising his eyebrows. Yet aside from this tower, he says, which actually isn't very old, and strictly speaking it would not in itself be a grand sight for us to see, there isn't much else. All right, Herr Doktor? he exclaims. What do you think? You'll come to the tower.

No, I say.

And why not, he asks.

Too far, I say.

But the tower, he says, you're wrong about it, the tower isn't as far away as you imagine. (How can he know how far away I imagine it to be?) So pull yourself together and come. Let's look at the tower!

No, I say.

And why not? he asks.

Too tired, I say, and yawn.

But now the supervisor suddenly maintains that there's nothing in the world so stimulating and refreshing as a walk through D., a walk to the tower.

In this heat, I exclaim.

Yes, even in this heat. Because the tower is outside the village, there are breezes there. You'll be amazed, he says, how the breezes blow where the tower is and how you'll not feel tired anymore when you set eyes on the tower. You'll take your head in both hands and ask yourself:

Why didn't I choose to go to the tower right away, why did I say no? Well, then, he says.

No, I say.

No? he asks.

No, I say.

And why not, he asks.

Yet I can't explain why. I just say: No, not to the tower! And that the whole proposal, the whole idea, is impossible for us. And already I'm on the verge of asking him, only so that he'll leave me sitting there, if, instead of going to the tower, he'd like to have a drink with me, but then it occurs to me that this would prolong his presence indefinitely, instead of shortening it, it would only increase the multitude of flies. So I don't ask him. Prefer to drink nothing myself, either, only so as not to have to invite him. Then he says he knows why we won't come.

Well, now, I say, so you know more than I do.

Yes, he says, but our fear that we might have to leap from ruin to ruin and drag ourselves from one monument to another was unfounded. There simply were no such ruins and monuments in D., except for the tower there was nothing, *nothing*. Thank God, I think, and with my hands, which reach to the floor, since I'm sitting—I'm a monkey in this situation, yes, a monkey!—I make a gesture, as if to say: That's it then. Why go on talking any longer, let's finish with this hogwash! But instead of drawing the right conclusion from this gesture, however vague it was, instead of ending the hogwash and with a bow leaving the dining room, where the air is thick and stale enough even without his presence, he suddenly exclaims: *Posso?* And with a subterranean droning sound he pulls a chair up, flicks to right and left his coattails up, and, without asking me or my wife, sits down with us at our table. So that, on account of this intrusiveness, I suddenly have the feeling that the man at our table isn't a supervisor at all, but something much worse. How often, as one is always reading, do stranded travelers take rooms in these small, inconspicuous hotels in the south—and are never seen again! Their plundered suitcases are found months later, even years later, in quite different parts of the country, but the travelers themselves, never. And it's of these travelers, who disappear in such regions, that I now can't help thinking. True, I'm still sitting, this afternoon, in this village of D., in company with my speechless wife, in the Hotel Lucia, and speaking with a man, that's to say, words are passing between us, I now have no idea what sort of words. But I keep telling myself that I should actually stand up and, arm in arm with my wife, run from the "dining room". And what if he wouldn't let us out through the door? Then we'd simply, as I now know, have to jump through the window, even if that meant cutting our faces to shreds. But we don't jump through the window. And it's due to the same lethargy which keeps me at this table, has kept me for seven years now, too, tied to my wife, child, profession, career. The analogies put me to shame, I'll skip them here, especially since my suspicion about the supervisor seems to me, almost immediately, to be idiotic. And I tell myself that my fears are taking me in the wrong direction. No, I'm thinking, not that direction, but the opposite one! And the person sitting with crossed arms

25

and legs at our table, I'm thinking, really is the supervisor here, who really does want to show us the tower. And that, in case something is up, something else, it's something you haven't found out about yet, something you probably haven't until now been able even to imagine.

3

The supervisor's appearance at such an awkward moment is certainly a coincidence, and an eerie one, too, because, just as he came in, I was wanting to tell my wife I'd decided to leave her. And why was I going to leave her? Not difficult to answer that. Incompatibility. And now—as if I hadn't secretly feared it for years—a child on the way. And indeed she told me of her pregnancy with exactly the same quiet, hesitant, and guilt-ridden words that I've always expected from her, words that for years I'd heard stealing up on me. Although deep down I know everything in advance, I freeze at once. Another child! Why not say now what has to be said in reply, say it now and here, the brutal truth? Thus on this very afternoon, after this speechless and grimly determined meal, with the unknown meat lying on her plate, in this totally foreign place, at the end of our holiday together, the last, as it now turns out. Yet whenever a truth is suddenly told, whenever a separation is decided on, a great misery takes hold of the person affected, of course. Even then, the truth must be told, the decision communicated. Awkward, though, that her pregnancy should make my decision seem characterless, which it isn't. Such a decision is, on the contrary, after the way our marriage has gone, perfectly natural. I've told her a hundred times, a thousand times, that another child would mean the end. So the wisest thing is to end our marriage now. First she had seduced me, then deceived, then tricked, and finally betrayed me, and for a long time I'd no longer loved, desired, needed her, et cetera; those are matters with which she could reproach me, or I her. Admit we can't go on like this for ever, I'd wanted to exclaim to her across the dishes, but I hadn't been able to, because the supervisor unexpectedly came in and later sat down. Short-legged, also short of breath, with his coat hanging open and his hair plastered to his skull, spreading the smell of brilliantine far into the empty room, he sits facing us and lets me see his sash. And he has placed on the table, between our glasses, his fleshy red hands, the paws of an animal not yet fathomed and defined, but a dangerous one. And since I can't endure seeing such things lying on our table and any announcement of my decision is now as good as impossible, I stand up, to the surprise of all, even to my own surprise, and exclaim that his references to the tower have made us—I say not *me* but *us*—inquisitive, and that we'd be willing, with his guidance, which certainly won't cost us the earth—here I laugh, I bleat—since for supervisors, I exclaim, there must be fees here, statutory fees, to see and tour the little town, the village, the place, briefly: D. and its tower, for he had made a convincing case. And I'm not thinking anymore about what he might be able to show us, in this burned-out interior of his island, but what else would we ever be able to do, how else should we spend the evening and night? Should each of us sit in a corner of his own in the low-ceilinged bedroom? Or perhaps here in the "dining room," the focus of a million swarming flies? Yet whatever we do this is the point at which we're lost, except that we don't yet know it. And I'm telling myself that once we've got the supervisor out of the "dining room" again, and have walked with him, arm in arm if necessary, around the *piazza,* we could certainly find some pretext to leave him outside the hotel and retreat into our room, lock ourselves in, and, if advisable, spend the time until morning alone, that's to say, together, behind the barricaded door. Then he'd clear off, he'd have to, disappear into the brawling of stray dogs. And I imagine the chair before me empty again, whereas in reality the supervisor is sitting there, short-legged, short of breath. Meanwhile my poor wife, slipping today from one fright to another, when I say that we will, after all, visit the place and the tower, naturally tries to protest, and in protest is raising her hands in a defensive gesture, but with one look I silence her. The supervisor reacts otherwise, the moment I stand up the blood goes to his head, with joy. He'd no longer been counting on compliance. *Grazie mille,* he exclaims, with a light in his eyes, and a shine on his cheeks. And at once he leaps up and hobbles at once to the door, but lets my wife, whom I lift from her chair and away from the table and have literally to push through the spacious echoing room, go through the door first. And he readies himself, first, though, as he passes, shouting into the smoke-blackened kitchen a message, a command, an admonition, in a dialect I don't understand, readies himself for his task, pulling over his round Sicilian skull a flat, round, black cap, the kind everyone wears here and which he had hitherto kept in his pocket.

Venga, venga, venga, he exclaims.

All right, we're coming, I say.

As we go out, down the corridor, I can take hold of the handle of our door and press it downward. And can tell: it's still locked! So we haven't been robbed, I'm thinking. *Not yet,* I'm thinking.

4

□ □

□

Then the heat outside, but that's nothing new, I've already described it. And, since it is one of the few intelligible things about these two days, it will have to be described again and again. For instance: it is African. For instance: a dry scorching wind like a blast of air from an oven, although the sea is not far off. Not a cloud in sight, only the sun and the sky, mindless, profound, violet. The light dazzling and piercing and unbroken, all colors garish and sharp. And the brilliant white of the crumbling walls, which of course makes a person of my sort think of bone ash. Briefly: in African light a landscape originally beautiful, perhaps ravishing, but now spoiled by a human presence, lapsed, ravaged, a landscape permeated with decay, ruins, and rubbish, unbearable. And me with the key in my right hand trouser pocket, the weight of it—soon a knife will be there—just in case of trouble with the supervisor. And the *piazza*, on a slightly higher level, slightly elevated in front of me. In spite of the sunlight, the brilliance, I feel I'm going into a theater, or up onto a stage.

Every tree, bush, even every vestige of the fountain—like a column, a sculpture, artifice, I mean, like a stage set. And the stillness theatrical and the sound of our footsteps staged. And I'm thinking that over the years nature here has been persistently touched up, reality trimmed and mitigated, and, with an all-embracing artistry, suppressed, but that now, as everything disintegrates, reality is coming to light again, through impoverishment. A reality that one can hardly measure up to, like any other reality, I'm thinking. And us now, all three of us, moving beside one another into this unbearable reality and across the *piazza*, around whose edges are cedars, cork trees, and cypress, all of them smutted with speckles that shade off into a rust color, and wooden benches, all of them collapsed, everywhere neglect, not only that, but everywhere piss and shit, it's true: if only there wasn't shit everywhere under one's feet. Then the pine, mentioned already, a tree with spreading branches. I take my wife by the arm. Of course she resists. After what I've "done" to her today—my second child, the child I kept secret!—she doesn't want me to touch her, not even by an elbow. Yet, as always, she doesn't resist for long. So I take her by the arm and guide her, not to the left, where the supervisor is shuffling along, but to the right, skirting the pine tree, so that I hide it from her, which is what I intend. For beneath the pine tree, in a yellow plastic basin, bled and chopped to pieces, its head mournfully set on its crossed thighbones, the goat is now lying. And the butchers, the children, all of them skinny, half-naked and ragged, dried by the wind and baked by the sun, silent, with bloody hands, stand around the basin, smoking. And it occurs to me that the goat could have been slaughtered perhaps, no, probably, on our account. And then it occurs to me: they've forgotten to skin it, the skin is still on the flesh. Or is the skin supposed to be a requisite for the cooking of the goat? And now the supervisor is shuffling past this yellow basin and calling out to the children the same—to me unintelligible—pronouncement or piece of information, the same command, the same enticement that he uttered when calling into the hotel kitchen. And they receive it with indifference, not responding, only the boy with the knife lowers his eyes. This small, sunny, gilded butcher: what a handsome boy! What shoulders, what hips! And I take hold of my wife more tightly, she is staring at the ground in front of her, and carefully I guide her, to protect her from any more bloody impressions, as if she were an invalid, around the basin. And I'm whispering into her ear that the whole thing isn't necessary and that it's my fault that we took this walk. And that I'll let her know, I'll tell her what I had been meaning to tell her after our meal when the supervisor had interrupted us, just as soon as this interruption is over, as soon as we've put an end to this farce of seeing the sights in a place where there's nothing to be seen. Things being as they are, it won't surprise you, and you won't like it, either, but, believe me, I tell her, you'll get over it, like everything else. And more, I hope you'll listen to me this time, I add, as soon as we're past the children and the basin. And I'm whispering in her ear that in this part of the world, as she must know, everything is done in the open, very crassly and very crudely and very visibly, and without any shame or decency. You know, I say, what I mean. I'm only reminding you now, I say, because behind us there's something you needn't see. So don't turn around. Listen, please don't look at the pine tree, don't look at the basin, I'm whispering, and at once she takes a look, of course.

O God, she exclaims, when she sees the basin and the children, who, cigarettes between their lips, are blowing the smoke in our direction, O God, she exclaims.

You see, I say, why don't you ever listen to me? That's something you might have spared yourself, like much else besides.

And thereupon the supervisor, who has heard everything, turns to us and says, by way of explanation: They're all downright animals.

I reply, not hiding my irritation: What?

Yes, he says.

I say, impatiently—for I'd like to move on more quickly and most of all right out the other side of the place, to stand in the shadow of the tower, which I imagine to be tall and round, and not always to be talking so much: What? How do you mean? Who?

The children, the children, he exclaims. Because they grow up, he says, and spreads his arms out as if to fly, together with the animals, like the animals, as indeed we can see for ourselves. Not good for them, he explains. Not good at all to be born into the world in D. or around it, because life here, *porca miseria*, is mostly a bad dream. To which one should, he says, put an end at the first opportunity, meaning—leave the place. And he waves his cane. For suddenly he has a cane, too (a walking stick), I don't know where he got it, because when he came to our table he didn't have one, I believe. But perhaps before he came in he had propped it against the wall outside. And as we left the hotel, while I was absorbed in the decay of the scenery, that's to say, with the perishing theatricality of the neighborhood, he had retrieved it, taken it into his hand, and now he's waving it in the air. And then, with the yellow basin behind us and almost forgotten, thanks to the climate, for the wind here makes one rapidly forget everything, again I'm saying, in my normal voice, thus loudly and firmly, in such a way as to arouse trust, and in a conversational tone, to the supervisor, but also to my wife, and to myself, no, to the whole world: We're astonished about many things here, no, I exclaim, we're horrified.

Aha, says the supervisor, slowing down a little, about what?

About what? About what? I exclaim. Well, can't you see?

No, he says, tell me.

All right, I say, for example the solitude, the desolation, the absence of people here. And it's true, it's as if D. had died. D. is empty. Hardly even a dog or cat to cross our path. Isn't it natural that, even if we don't speak of it, we should be horrified at this desolation, this dilapidation, and that we should keep on thinking of it, except when we're thinking of her pregnancy or his tower? Isn't everything here, all the way up the hill and far down into the valley, like a dead place, I exclaim. And how to explain it, is it even explainable. And at once, since I've read a bit about the region, I also have two theories ready, one sociological, one geological, but I'm not telling them yet, later perhaps. But now since we've covered a fair distance along the "High Street," which is neither paved nor asphalt, has no other surface either, and which . . . No! I won't describe it. And we've been walking in silence up this street, without perceiving, either in front of the houses or inside them, any people or traces of people—no voices, movement, smoke, light, noise—just as, in front of our hotel and inside it, except for the cook who gave us our key and served our meal, we've not seen, heard, *perceived* any people or signs of people, only the butchers, the children. And as for the "houses" here, I'm thinking . . . As for the houses here, I say, they are . . .

I know what they are, exclaims the supervisor and waves me away. You needn't tell me.

And how, I ask, can you live here?

But we can't, of course, he says.

And how, I ask, would you describe the houses?

Perhaps in disrepair, he says.

Disrepair, I exclaim, and I laugh.

Or else, he says, inserting between his lips a cheap cigarette of black Alpha tobacco, ruined.

Yes, I say, and so ready for demolition that for us it's difficult to guess whether they're still inhabited or were forgotten long ago. Now, supervisor, I exclaim, are they still inhabited, yes or no?

Aha, he says, and lights the cigarette, so it's a good thing that you took me along with you after all, isn't it? You must be grateful to me now, don't you think? And he laughs and comes so close to me that I can see the threads of tobacco hanging in the corners of his mouth. For without him, he says, as I gently push him away, we'd be lost as regards any understanding of the situation. And he explains to us, as he stops and with a gesture invites us also to take a rest: D., like many places hereabouts, is still indicated on the maps and mentioned in documents, but in fact it ceased to exist quite some time ago. It exists, yet it doesn't exist, if I know what he . . .

What you mean? I ask.

What I think, he says.

So then D. is deserted, I thought so, I exclaim. Did you hear that, Maria, I say, and I walk up to the nearest house and, to convince myself it is deserted, knock with my fist several times rapidly on the wall, and indeed it sounds hollow and empty. And now I'm wanting to ask about the children, whom I suddenly recall, in this context of horrible desolation, and where do these children live (sleep, eat, have their homes) and why is it they who slaughtered the goat, and if it is usual here for children to slaughter animals outside the hotel windows while smoking cigarettes, but here he interrupts me. You're wrong, he says, earnestly, the houses aren't empty, I never said that.

Not empty then? I ask.

No, he says, not empty.

Even though it sounds so hollow? I ask.

Hollow, perhaps, he says, but not empty. Because the authorities have so far managed . . . he goes on and opens his coat, so that the red sash he's wearing becomes visible again. And I'm thinking: Aha, now he wants to show you that he's associated with the authorities, perhaps he is the authorities, and I point at the sash and say in a respectful voice: The authorities, aha, the authorities! Quite correct, he says, that is so. Well, then: Through measures which were all aimed at opening the region to tourism, that being the most principle aim of all, they had managed to restrain, at least for the meantime, most of the inhabitants from leaving, that's to say: from going overseas for ever. There's still hope, he says, because the authorities had spread hope around. Except that previously they'd sought salvation in the earth . . .

Yes, indeed, I exclaim, the catacombs.

. . . But then, he goes on, the antique marbles and other things for which they'd dug had not appeared, so that now, if one might say so . . .

But surely, I exclaim, but of course . . .

. . . Now, he says, we've set our hopes, so to speak, on the air.

You mean? I ask.

Yes, indeed, he says, and brandishes his cane.

And how, I ask, how do you mean, if one may ask . . .

Quite simply this, he says, and with his cane he sketches in the dust where we're standing something steeply erect, high, pointed. You know what it is? he asks.

The tower, I ask.

Yes, he says, the tower. That's what our hopes are set on, everyone's. At this very moment, people are sitting in their houses, hoping. Except that they don't show themselves.

You mean there are people here still, I ask.

Yes, he says, that's right.

You mean, I ask, inside this house. And I knock once more against the wall of the house.

Come and see for yourself, he says. And he goes to the tiny half-opened window of the house and beckons me over. And since I'm so close to the house myself—I won't describe it—and have knocked a few times against the wall, however lightly, with my fist, I obey and follow him to the window, which he pushes open for me, inward. And when I hesitate, out of a sort of respect or shyness, which restrains me from looking into the house, strange as it is and yet evidently inhabited, he presumes to one of the confidences I'd been fearing. Before I can stop him, he simply grasps the back of my neck with his undefined but warm paw and simply pushes my head through the window, into the house.

Hey! what are you doing, stop it, I exclaim, hearing what I've said in the sound, in the echo of my voice, inside the house. And I try to shake away his hand, which not only disgusts me but also hurts. But, *signor*, I'm not doing anything to you, only drawing your attention to something peculiar, the supervisor exclaims, so forcefully that the spittle flies from his mouth. Do you see? he asks, and he relaxes his grip somewhat.

See? I exclaim, but what am I supposed to see?

But, *signor*, he exclaims, you yourself asked about it.

See? I exclaim, but what am I supposed to see?

Well, he says, the answer to your question, of course.

And what was my question, I exclaim.

Whether the place is still inhabited, of course, that's what, he says, and puffs on his cigarette.

See, I exclaim again, and how am I supposed to see anything when you're pressing on my neck like that? And in fact I've been much too busy twisting and turning my neck, trying to free it from his grip, to have been able to *see* anything.

There, he exclaims, into the room, you could say into both rooms. The house actually has only one room, so both rooms are the same. It's called a *dammuso,* it has one door and only one window, if any at all. The whole family lives in it, together with the animals, if there are animals. Do you see it now, he asks.

See? I exclaim, but what am I supposed to see? And there's only one thought in my head: How can you free your poor neck from his grip?

È be, that, of course, he says, and points over my shoulder into a corner of the *dammuso.* Where I do actually see, once my eyes have got used to the darkness of the low, narrow, and evil-smelling room and peered around with my head stretched out, more or less separate from the rest of me, it's hanging across into another world, on an iron rod built into the wall beside the door, like rare birds in a darkened cage, four or five or six skinny old women, lips peeled back over toothless gums, cheeks hollow and shrunken, their scraggy, fleshless necks, on which too many folds of skin are hanging, stretched out, as if they meant to

40

sing, crouching there motionless and staring into space. I'm startled, deeply so, of course. And after the most various thoughts have shot in the most various directions through my head, I have for a moment the extraordinary impression that the figures in the *dammuso,* in a way that I can't yet quite comprehend, must have been made artificially, or they must be dead. Yes, I'm thinking, either artificial or dead. Yet because I'm not sure and I don't want to make a fool of myself, I don't mention this first impression to the supervisor for the time being. I don't even tell it aloud to my wife, who has stayed standing on the road, but keep it, for now, to myself. I only ask: What is it?

Aha, he exclaims, are you interested?

Yes, I say, what is it. You can safely tell me.

Well, he says, deliberately or not tickling my ear a bit with his little finger, it's the previous inhabitants of the house, of course. They must have fallen asleep. And with these words he finally, finally, lets go of my neck.

Fallen asleep, I exclaim and quickly draw my liberated head back out of the *dammuso.* And since I'm still thinking that the figures are either dead or artificial, thus made of a material elsewhere unknown and possibly only available here, let's say, the parts carved or turned on a lathe, and then inserted into one another, hung with loose, broad, black lengths of cloth and set on the rod, I ask, wiping the sweat from my forehead, if the German word *eingeschlafen* might not have to be understood in a special way, *à la sicilienne,* at least not in the usual way, perhaps?

For an Italian, I say, you speak an exceptionally good German, and one can tell that you've spent many years in Frankfurt, but now and again you use words—for instance, this word *eingeschlafen*—in such a way as to change the usual sense. Well then, I exclaim, and knock several times against the wall, tell me how the word *eingeschlafen* has to be understood hereabouts.

Well, it's because of the heat, of course, the supervisor replies, and now that he too is mindful of the heat, he wipes the sweat from his forehead. You feel the heat too, don't you? Surely one doesn't have to explain that to you?

No, no, I certainly feel the heat, I say, and for a moment I suspect again that the supervisor is making fun of me.

Listen, I then exclaim, after peering once more, this time of my own accord, far into the *dammuso,* and pulling my head back out again, probably my eyesight isn't as good as it was, but unfortunately I can't quite identify what's in there. But I'm very interested in what it is, yes indeed, believe me.

Aha, the supervisor says and taps the house several times with his cane, so you're glad after all that I came along with you?

Of course, I say, this is all new to me.

That's true, he says, even in Palermo Cathedral one seldom sees anything like this.

Yes, I say, but what is it? I'm none the wiser. Of course, one gets ideas, one wonders about this and that, but . . .

You're in the dark, he asks.

Yes.

Good, he says. Excellent, he says.

Why, I ask.

Because, he says, that's where I can help you.

Yes, I say, nothing could be better.

Well, then, he says, what do you want to know?

Right, I say, first of all there's especially one thing that would interest me. Even if for you seeing that you're at home here and know what goes on behind the scenes, the question might seem a bit strange.

Ask, ask, he exclaims.

Well, it's this, I say. But allow for the fact that I'll have to simplify the question somewhat.

You can ask your question, the supervisor says, in whatever way suits you best.

But it sounds, I say, when I put it in such a simplified way, somewhat unusual, if not silly.

It doesn't matter, he says.

All right, then, put simply and directly, the question is this, I say. Are they people or not, are they alive or are they dead?

Well, the supervisor says, and my question seems not to bother him, with a faint smile: They're people, of course, what did you think? People who are, on the one hand, still alive, he says, while on the other hand they've been dead for a long time.

So they're not artificial, I ask.

No, he says, after a pause for reflection, during which he wipes his forehead with his coat sleeves, once right and once left, they're not artificial.

43

Aha, I say. For a moment I thought they were, but the impression must have been due to the heat. You know, we're simply not used to such heat.

I know, he says. And after a little pause, he again says: No, they're not artificial. Although, if one thinks about it a bit, one might consider them so, and those *rod people*, in their own thoughts and reflections, have probably considered themselves so—perhaps as artificial, or even as dead.

Do they still think about it, I ask.

Well, whether or not they think is not something one can tell from the outside, the supervisor says, but it's possible they do.

And how long, I ask, have they been sitting there?

Oh, a long time, a very long time, the supervisor says, after a pause for thought. Some for as long as thirty, perhaps forty, yes, almost fifty years. And hardly ever going out. You know that they're women, so to speak, he asks.

I thought so.

Yes, he says, they are, or at least they were women, whose husbands died, or were killed, thirty or forty or fifty years ago.

Killed, I exclaim, look . . .

Yes, unfortunately, he says, scratching his neck. Not so that it took anyone by surprise, and not all at once, but gradually, if that's the right way to put it. They were all peasants, in those days. First their water was drained away, then the well was poisoned, then the barn was set on fire, and then the cow had a leg sawn off, always a hind leg, always the left leg, and finally . . . Well, finally . . .

44

Aha, I say. But how . . . But that's . . . Maria, I exclaim, sticking my head into the *dammuso* quickly once again, as the ghastliness of this whole spectacle gradually dawns on me, Maria, come over here quickly, see what an interesting room this gentleman is showing us. It's called a *dammuso* and isn't in any of the guidebooks. Not one, I exclaim, it certainly isn't. But since one is here one can look inside. Right beside the door there's a rod, with something perched on it, probably women. Some for as long as fifty years, imagine, without moving. First their husbands' wells were poisoned, then they were killed, but it hasn't ever been proved. And they never go out into the fresh air, either, do they? I ask the supervisor.

That's true, unfortunately they seldom come out to take the air, he says, brushing a few flies aside, actually almost never.

Do you hear what he says, Maria, I exclaim. And imagine, as long as they've never gone out they haven't had any thoughts. But the bit about the thoughts isn't proved, it's only supposed. The result, as the gentleman here says, is that they're neither dead nor alive.

Ah, the gentleman, what's this? this supervisor exclaims and he makes a dismissive gesture. I'm Giovanni, but you can call me Herr Hans, if you like. And you, *signora*, he says, turning to my wife, don't be timid, come and look into the *dammuso*, too, it's quite safe. And for the *rod people* it can only be helpful, if they're looked at, they'll have to get used to it. And now standing there, feet wide apart, with his cane held between his legs, he tells us: These are the oldest women in D., who all without excep-

45

tion belonged to the unfortunate class of the *Cat Eaters* and whom someone has put here for us, all in one heap, perched on the rod. But he won't say who.

Ah, I say, waving him away, you don't have to tell us, we know.

Well, he says, so you know. And who put them on the rod?

You yourself, of course, who else, I exclaim.

But the supervisor, who for some reason won't admit to putting the women on the rod for us, makes a dismissive gesture. You think so? is all he says. And then, since he has promised, he begins to explain everything to us. That the women had lived collectively three hundred and eighty-five years and given birth to seventy-three children, of whom they had immediately lost fifty-nine, most of them in tragic circumstances. For example, Signora Sale, the one to the left of the door, had had to let two of her eleven children, only girls, however, go into the formerly copious river, because she hadn't been able to feed all eleven of them. And the woman with the fan, Signora Farina, had even lost—a much more tragic case—two grown sons, one killed with a shotgun, the other with a knife. So we needn't be surprised at their being so fossilized. It was particularly tragic in their case that both sons had died for politics—the opposite sides of that time, so that, in a sense, they had killed one another. Now she always has their photographs with her. And had I seen the photos in her lap?

Yes, of course, I say, although it was much too dark in the

dammuso, of course, for me to have seen them. In any case, the supervisor tells us, fanning himself with the flat of a hand, they creep together here at noon and take a rest from their individual tragedies, which most of them have forgotten, anyhow.

So they don't even suffer anymore, I ask.

Yes, yes, he says, they suffer all right. But not for a definite reason anymore, more from habit, in a quite general way.

And they've forgotten the details?

Forgotten everything, he exclaims, everything. That's why I had to reflect for such a long time, before I could answer your question whether they're still alive. And then quickly he draws my attention to their glossy hair, into which, as has been since time immemorial the custom here, they have rubbed for our benefit animal fats, which make the hair easier to comb and braid. And then, turning once more to my wife: Just take a look at their hair, *signora*, that will interest you, as a woman.

But my wife, because of the heat or actual timidity or because she feels unwell or wants to spite me or wound me, refuses to come to the window and look into the *dammuso*. No, she says, I don't want to, no. But you can just take a look, I say, it doesn't matter.

No, she says, I don't want to see.

So what do you want, I ask.

I want to go home.

Where does the *signora* want to go, the supervisor asks.

Home, I say, back to the hotel.

But that's impossible, he exclaims, we're going to the

47

tower, has she forgotten? Come on, he says, and takes me by the sleeve, let's go to the tower.

Don't worry, we're coming, you don't have to drag me by the sleeve, I say. And you needn't be troubled by what my wife says. She's in a bad mood, that's all. In a bad mood, the supervisor says to my wife, you shouldn't be in a bad mood. And not looking into the *dammuso* is only your own loss, because it's as instructive as it is interesting, and not harmful. Besides, they were all asleep.

Don't take any notice of her, I say, making a dismissive gesture, she's upset. And it was because of me that she hadn't wanted to look into the *dammuso*. That's to say, she had done something rather silly, to annoy me, so that we weren't on good terms at the moment. That was why she wouldn't listen to me now, that was why she wanted to punish me. Isn't that so, dear, you want to punish me? I say to my wife, but she doesn't answer.

Oh well, that's how it goes, the supervisor says, and he strokes his chin, which, like his hair, is scented. And then it occurs to him that one could photograph the *dammuso* and the *rod people*. So the *signora* could look at the pictures later on, when we'd made friends again. One could also show them to acquaintances and point out to them what interesting photographic subjects were to be found in D., even though the place was still quite undeveloped touristically. He could imagine that a photograph taken through the window . . .

Or not? he asks.

No, I say, I don't want to.

48

If it's because of the dark, he says, the *rod people* can be moved closer to the window.

No, it's not because of the dark, but . . . I just don't want to, I say, and push his suggestion aside, for I've decided not to photograph the *rod people*. And then I push him aside, too, he's breathing much too freely in my face. And I'm asking myself if my wife isn't perhaps right to want to go home, I mean: to the hotel.

For, actually, I say and look at my watch, but no sooner do I see it than I recall that on our arrival here, probably on the ferry, it suddenly stopped and I've been having the greatest difficulty in telling the time since then, but I don't tell the supervisor this. Instead I say: I see it's later than I thought. Actually we should be going home. Especially since we've now seen a few things. Yes, I say, let's go back!

Go back? the supervisor exclaims, and he straightens up, shocked. Then he shakes his head, violently. But that's quite impossible.

Why impossible?

No, he says, no turning back. We'll go now, he says, to the tower, let's leave the *rod people*. It's time we went to the tower, he exclaims, and he claps his hands.

And why the tower, I ask.

Because of the spectacle, he says.

And what sort of spectacle will it be, I ask.

Yes, indeed, he says.

And why, I ask, should it be *us* that are going to your spectacle. Why, I ask, don't you try it with someone else from among the hundreds, or thousands, of tourists who spend the whole summer, if not exactly in D., then certainly nearby, lying in the sun and roasting themselves? And who would all, I say, relish nothing more than to go with you to the tower, if someone asked them to. Yes, they'd even climb up the tower with you—but we're quite certainly not the right people for that. Can't you see how exhausted we are? And in this state we're supposed to . . . you want us to . . .

Yes, indeed, he says shuffling his feet on the ground, to the tower.

What do you mean, I exclaim. What presumption, forcing us to walk in this heat through a village without a scrap of shade, subjecting us to this entirely unnecessary strain. Just see how we're sweating, I exclaim, and point to my forehead. So if I'm saying: in this state, then I know what I'm talking about. What nonsense, always to be insisting on this tower, considering I've told you we don't want it at all. Why don't you leave us in peace and go on your own? If this spectacle is as unique as you say, nobody will notice our absence. There'll be a big enough crowd, even without us. You're only wasting your time with us, always talking about this tower and trying to lure us to a place and to get us involved in something . . .

Yes, indeed, he says, to the tower.

All right, I tell myself, to the tower! So that you'll finally see the tower you're all this time really so curious about, and know how high, old, ruined, et cetera, it is. So that you won't always have to be asking yourself why you're thinking of the tower, but have it manifest before you, and then, just as soon, behind you. Perhaps you'll just take a quick photograph of it and then, I'm thinking, then . . .

And then, who knows, perhaps even in the shadow of this tower, the announcement of your decision to leave her, the decision you've been pushing around inside your head for such a long time. For in fact I do keep pushing around inside my skull the phrases in which I'll be clothing this decision. And I'm thinking that this can't go on, and that . . . and that . . . and that . . .

Well, the supervisor says, at least you now know that, contrary to all appearances, most of the people of D. are still here. They're hidden in the houses, and since today's the day, they're waiting and hoping and praying for tourists to come and for these tourists to . . .

I know, I say, it's the spectacle. And I make, even then, a slip of the tongue and instead of saying: People at the tower, I say: People in the catacombs. Ah yes, I say, as we walk side by side back on to the street, the *catacombs* will be on view today.

No, he shouts, stopping in his tracks and stamping his feet, wrong! Oh get along with you, he exclaims, you're not even listening. Not the catacombs! The tower, the tower! Ah yes, I say, sorry. The tower, I say, of course, the tower.

Yes, indeed, he says, the tower. As for the catacombs, make no mistake, he exclaims, gripping my arm, listen, you must forget about them completely, they're lost and gone for ever. But there are other ways and means to bring visitors

51

to D., *gli stranieri,* who want to see and experience something extraordinary, and pay for it. Even if, he adds, since you've no conception of the misery and distress hereabouts, you can't imagine these ways and means, either. But then everything is unimaginable to you in this part of the world.

5

□ □

□

The village of D. before us—no, we're in the middle of it—
is situated on the slopes of a hilly landscape which, formed
over thousands of years by tectonic movements, is sprinkled
with erratic blocks and grooved with gullies: an instance
of *faulting*, with the typical signs of frequent earthquakes,
earth tremors, vulcanism. So our way to the tower goes
alternately up and down, and my wife—but me too, even
me—we're soon out of breath. And this village, which, as
one can see from its collapsing and crumbling ornamental
façades (baroque) and from the stucco on the upper walls
and attics and balconies of the better houses, must have
been a pretty and prosperous market town, is now the contrary. There's an empty window frame, for example, clack-
ing in the wind.
It's nothing, the supervisor says, pay no attention to that.
Many doors, windows too, are boarded up, but even these
boards are weathered and warped or wrenched away. Then
we come to an old church, but where is its tower? When I

53

ask the supervisor, he stands leaning into the scorching wind, makes a slight bow to me, and apologizes about the church tower, but nobody knew where it was. It must have simply collapsed one day, he says.

Collapsed, I exclaim.

Quite correct, he says.

Well now, I say. And kick a small stone, now to the left, now to the right, in front of me, as I walk along. Not a person anywhere to be seen! But the marks of people, here and there, signs that people could be living here. A wooden plow, for instance, in a dark vault, where there are also some boards, an old pair of boots beside the boards, and, in front of a door, a cart with flowerpots in it, but empty ones. And over there, says the supervisor, putting his left hand on his member, is the *Mortality Association.*

The what? I exclaim.

That's what it's called, he says.

And when, as is possible sometimes, we look through the gaps between the houses, we see far into an open countryside, with fig trees, cactus, magnolias, palms, oleander, mimosa. Later, there's a slope we go up, the supervisor between us, the red sash between us, but also the argument with my wife about the children, the *child,* between us, the child I don't want to have put into the world. But I've long since shifted this argument to the interior of my thoughts. In my thoughts, on their inner edges, I'm thus saying to my wife: Whether we stay together or not, you yourself should have seen how necessary it is to get rid, as quickly as possible, of this *unwanted thing* which is trying to come between us and our happiness, I can only wonder at your being so slow about it. And that, once it's all over, she should give herself a treat, a reward, for instance have a really good sleep for once. For neither she nor I have been able, since arriving on the island, to sleep properly, really to *fall asleep.* Who knows, I propose to say, perhaps the doctor will give you something to make you relax, so that you'll feel, if only for a while, better, even happy.

While I'm having this talk with myself, we come to an alley *(vicolo)* which differs from the main street only in being—if that were possible—even more thick with filth. That's to say, the house walls are even more thickly smeared and bespattered with filth, the roofs even more ramshackle and holed, and there's even more excrement by the doorways, so that, just about as the word *happy* comes to my mind, my wife suddenly wants to throw up.

Feeling sick, I ask.

Yes, she says.

All right, I take her by the arm and guide her toward a corner. Must get it out, I say. And: You can deal with it here, nobody's looking, I say, and push her into the corner, while the supervisor walks on a few steps ahead. And then she does her level best, while I walk in a semicircle around her, with the cameras, my hands in my pockets, taking long strides. And eventually I'm standing behind her and from time to time—she's bending far over—hold her hands and, because of the stink—it's a corner for defecation—have to light a cigarette and keep it in my mouth. And resolve to tell the supervisor that this is enough, no more proposals on his part, no more sick-making sightseeing for us—he has stepped aside, with his back to us he's drawing some sort of figure in the filth with his cane, but I can't see what. But then again I'm thinking: the tower. Perhaps you really should first take a look at it. For, even after seeing the *dammuso*, the tower, I don't know why, has been on my mind. Yes, even while I've been thinking that the pregnancy must be ended, I've been thinking of the tower. And since the supervisor is silent and my wife is being miserable in the corner, I suddenly have a clear idea of the spectacle at the tower, with flags fluttering from the top of it, to enliven the impression, but also below, around the tower. And the people, the *Cat Eaters*, have crept out of their *dammusi* and have also brought flags, they're running around the tower, waving their flags. A people's festival is being simulated, that's how I imagine it. Until my wife, emptied, comes out of her corner.

I want to go back, she says.

Back, I ask, why?

To the hotel, she says.

And why to the hotel, I ask.

I want, she says, to lie down.

Lie down, I exclaim, now, in that terrible room?

Yes, she says, I want to lie down.

Later, I say.

So that instead of turning back—it would still have been possible—we walk on, up the hill. Before she was sick we had walked all three together, over this frightful island, sometimes keeping step, side by side on a broad front, but now that she's been sick we let the supervisor, obsessed by the idea of showing us his tower, walk in front of us. A sedate personality, in trousers that are much too tight, too shiny, with too high a gloss, as we now also notice from behind. My wife and I follow him, she clinging to me, gripping my arm with her fingernails. She has now, quite of her own accord, given me the arm she'd refused me till now, in her disgust at the child of mine I hadn't told her about. And once more, in order to calm her down, I've assured her that I hadn't wanted this child, but that it had come into the world against my will, all because of its calculating mother, who had perhaps wanted to get a husband for herself. And so as to establish a new feeling of fellowship between us, I whisper to her that I too detest this tour of the village of D. and would rather turn back, but I add that it would be injudicious to offend the supervisor, who is "probably an unpredictable and moody person, he might also be quick-tempered and dangerous," and to cut short our walk before reaching the tower.

And this tower, you know, quite frankly, I'd like to see it, I say.

And for her benefit, although she says nothing and doesn't want to see it—probably nothing in the world interests her less—I portray the tower as I picture it to be, as the one stable point in a landscape dissolving in the heat. And I explain to her that a return to the hotel, and she knows what it's like, just think how it would be at night with the *piazza* and its nauseous horrors darkening outside the window, would certainly be no improvement. Remember how it is, I exclaim.

No, she says, I don't want to remember.

You see, I say. And then continue, more or less as follows: Certainly what we'd seen so far on our walk and were still seeing and perhaps would see, was horrible, will be horrible, but who can guarantee that what we'll see in our hotel and the experiences we'll have there will be any less so? Perhaps things inside and in front of the hotel would be even more horrible than things on our walk. Anyway, nobody could guarantee the opposite. And it's like this, too, I add, and hesitate for a while, wondering how to say it, until I say, more or less: her own present circumstances, they were the reason for her being shocked and finding *everything* horrible now, it wasn't because of the misery all around. For me, I say, it's different. For me, and I've seen more of the world, and am perfectly familiar with conditions on three continents, things are only tiresome or a burden, but for her they're shocking or tragic. Till now she'd been just a dreamer, pampered by life, for whom the cold space of the world, when it suddenly opened up before her, was doubly terrifying. For me it was nothing new. And even the *Cat Eaters* had got used to a lot of things, even to everything, and were reconciled to their fate, if not content with it. What I mean to say, I whisper to her, as we walk on, is that they don't suffer anymore, for which one should actually give thanks to God. For our hope, that in the course of a gradual improvement in global circumstances, their circumstances would improve too, had turned out to be a historical mistake during the last few years, if we're honest about it. Hope, I exclaim, there is no hope for them, quite the contrary. The one interesting thing now is not the question whether they'll be oppressed, but how much deeper their oppression can go. Yes, I say, sometimes one would like to know how much deeper it can go.

At this the supervisor stops suddenly, and after whacking at a rat with his cane, waits for us. It had come out of a crack in a wall, so close that we could clearly see its heart beating. (Very strong and fast, the little rat heartbeat.) And he asks us, when we've caught up with him, if he might now walk beside us again, because we'd soon be coming to a square which used to be the marketplace, *mercato,* and he'd have to explain it to us.

Explain the market, I exclaim, and can't suppress a smile.

Yes, he says, and the Foundlings' Home.

And the tower, I exclaim, have you forgotten the tower?

Don't worry, he says, I won't forget it.

And where is it, your tower, I ask, when will it finally come? Don't you see how curious about it you've made us? Well, he says, brushing a finger across his mustache, not without pride, the tower comes later.

Later, always later, I exclaim, why not now? And why hadn't he told us right away that the tower was so far away, so high up on the hill. And in this heat, not a cloud in the sky, and us completely exposed to it, we would give something for a gust of wind, a little one, cool. And whether under these conditions, I say, and I'm meaning to ask him whether we couldn't see the tower first and only afterward, if necessary still, the market and the Foundlings' Home, but he won't even let me ask my question.

59

No, *signor*, he says with surprising firmness and resolve, first the Foundlings' Home, then the market, and then, if it's convenient, the tower.

All right, I say.

6

□ □

□

The Foundlings' Home, on which he sets such value, and
which he proceeds to show us, taking a few steps and stopping again, legs apart, his cane pointing at a two-storied
building set back somewhat on the right-hand side of the
street, a building that was once painted in bright colors
but is now weathered, darkened, become dingy, behind a
wall chest-high in a neglected garden, weeds up to one's
knees, itself orphaned, so to speak, was constructed, he explains, as we walk to the gateway and peer through the
grating, in the eighteenth century, and had been a partly
private, partly ecclesiastical foundation, and in use until
quite recently. *Tutto questo funzionava*, he exclaims and
points through the door with his cane. And into this Foundlings' Home, he tells us—while I'm cursing him, for why
must he talk to us now about a Foundlings' Home. I ask
myself, just when my wife is pregnant and the child mustn't
be born and we're on the verge of separation?—here it
was that for decades all unwanted children, all *superfluous*
children, were brought, he says, and he points toward the

garden. You must forgive me, he continues, turning to my wife, his hand on his heart, for my use of the phrase "superfluous children," *signora*, but it's an exact translation of the local dialect word. We'd really have to forgive him anyway for his blunt way of speaking, but in Frankfurt he'd learned to express himself in a direct and forthright way, instead of in metaphors and images and poetic turns of speech that would have better suited him. And then actually there always had been very many superfluous children here, and things hadn't changed at all. Because, he says, people are, so to speak, soaked in sexuality, you'll forgive the expression, he exclaims, because sexuality here is the only basis and proof of life, of existence.

Incidentally: How many children did the *signora* have?

I at once take a step forward to answer the question myself. One child, I say.

Only one, he exclaims, and he raises his eyebrows.

Yes, one.

And is it a boy, he asks, or otherwise?

Otherwise, I say. And repeat once more: One child, yes, one child.

Well, he says, the *signora* is still young. There'll be babies to come yet. All right, he then says with a gloomy expression: The putting away of children.

The what, I exclaim.

I'll explain it now, he says.

Obviously, I say, it's again something that . . .

Yes, he says, it's not to be seen.

Something ghastly, I ask.

Yes, he says, *con l'imaginazione*.

Is it necessary, I ask.

Yes, and historic, he exclaims. You see, it was here—and he beckons us to come closer. Closer? We still hesitate. Closer, please, closer, he exclaims. All right, then, closer. The understandable wish of the putters-away was respected, he continues, in so far as here—and that's the historic thing, he exclaims, look! And he walks to the high, warm wall, which, as we see, has green bottle fragments stuck along the top, but is otherwise decaying and crumbling, and close to the ground is enlivened by lizards. And he beckons us closer still. Good, and still closer. Slowly and cautiously, my wife on my arm, left hand on my cameras, I obey him and am telling myself: You'll go to the wall, but no farther. There's nothing to worry about, I'm telling myself, just go to the wall and take a look at whatever it is, because everything is historic now. And because at any time, if he shows us something unendurable, we can turn away, give him his tip, and walk off. Yes, I'm thinking, at anytime you can cut this whole thing short and go away, back to the hotel. And forget it all, I'm thinking, as I walk up to the wall.

It was here, he says, all three of us now in a row facing the wall, and he points to an opening right beside the door, about chest-high, and set in the wall, to this opening here, he says, look, it's just big enough for a nursling, the *superfluous children,* mainly just after they were born, were brought and pushed through. But now pay attention, he exclaims. For it turned out that there were many more *superfluous children* among them than anyone had supposed when the home was built and the hole put in. Not

63

only in this area but in the surrounding country, word went about that there was a hole here *into which one can push them*. Whereupon the mothers, also the fathers, came from all directions, people who, whatever their reason, wanted to get rid of their children in an inconspicuous and bloodless way, but not only the newborn ones. So that until recently also three- and four-year-olds, even five-year-olds—well, perhaps I'm exaggerating a bit here— were forced through this opening, into which you can put your hand, *signora*, if you like, it won't hurt, he says, to my wife, pointing at the hole, and this meant harming them, even mutilating the children. But you'll have seen as much for yourselves, just imagine, that the children must be harmed and mutilated, he exclaims, moving the cane, with which he's just driven the rat away, around in the hole, which is really very small. A child perhaps four years old, perhaps five, to put it into an opening like this, just imagine, he exclaims. Head and shoulders wouldn't fit in, at that age. And a child's head, when it's forced into such a hole, would *have* to be damaged, at least badly grazed. I ask you, *signora*, he exclaims, adopting his favorite posture, legs apart and cane between them, and turning once more to my wife, would you allow your five-year-old child, head first to be . . . No no no, I exclaim, gesturing to him to stop, let's hear no more of it.

Why, he exclaims, just let me ask.

Not necessary, I exclaim.

Because there is no such child? he asks.

Superfluous, I exclaim.

Because there's no child of that age, he asks.

No, not at all, I exclaim, but because such questions only lead to all sorts of misunderstandings, I say, and place my arm around my wife's shoulder, drawing her to me. Ah, I'm thinking, why didn't we stay on the autostrada?

All right, then, he says, walking around us and then talking to us from the other side, just supposing the *signora* had such a child, even if she actually hasn't, at least not one of that age. Would you, if it was of that age, allow it— this is only a question—to be pushed head first into this hole here? *Coraggio, signora,* he says, tell me.

Stop it now, I exclaim and stamp my foot a little, that's enough.

Perchè? he asks

Because we've understood, I exclaim.

But the supervisor won't let up. He shifts, from the other side now, closer to my wife, who suddenly has livid marks on her face, especially on her forehead and temples, and so she really is pregnant, or . . .? And he blows hot-mouthed his next question into her face. Would she rather do it herself, shove the bambino into this hole here?

And my wife, pale, the color drained from her face, the marks even more livid, retreating, turns to me: What does he want?

Don't listen to him, I say, don't answer.

Just look, he says, just look! And he spreads his arms, as he'd done when he first appeared.

Then I step in between him and her and push him back, my arm, with which till now I've been shielding the cameras, jabbing him in the chest, I push him away from her toward the door, the grating. That's enough now, I say.

The supervisor, feeling the blow, at once apologizes. We'd misunderstood. The whole conversation, the whole subject, had been a misunderstanding, but not his fault. He'd left Frankfurt so long ago that it was as if his German had evaporated. Whatever he might say now wouldn't be understood. I open my mouth, he exclaims, as usual, but what comes out is the contrary. I'm always asking, he exclaims, the wrong question. And saying the wrong word, he exclaims. Or had he gone too close to the *signora fisicamente,* he wants to say. Had he perhaps blown on her, with his mouth? And he holds his hand, his *paw,* in front of his mouth, his *maw,* I tell myself. For he'd never meant to breathe on anyone, least of all on the *signora.*

Forget it, I say and gesture him away.

No, he says, I have to know.

Let's talk of other matters, I say.

No, he exclaims, *per cortesia.* Just so that he can assure us—at this point I'm afraid he might fall to his knees—that he couldn't go on living, if he didn't know we'd forgiven him.

Yes, yes, I say, all right.

Forgiven, he exclaims.

Let's say no more of it, I say.

Then he places his arms on my shoulders and presses me to his breast. *Bene,* he says, settled. All the same, he says, letting me go, he must insist that everything he says or has said or will say during the course of the day or of days to come, even if it came out wrong, or had come out wrong, was the purest truth, and there wasn't a word of exaggeration in it, and that in D. there really were people who *still to this day* suffered from mutilations, mainly of the head, which they'd incurred when being put away into the hole in the Annunciata Foundlings' Home. And who, to this day, he exclaims, curse the little hole through which they'd had to pass at the start of their lives, also the pair of hands, the ones that pushed them in as well as the ones that pulled them out on the other side. . . . And that, if we liked, this evening, before or after the spectacle, he could bring these people to us, introduce them, show them . . .

I, with a gesture as emphatic as I can make it: Stop it now, I exclaim, no, no, no!

7

□ □

□

Whereupon we quickly set off again, I might say rush off, both crimson in the face and without viewing the Foundlings' Home from the other side, where supposedly there's a window frame worth seeing (baroque), and this time I walk in the middle. All right then, so we're going to the tower, I'm hoping. My early impression that the smell of carrion hanging over the island has been getting more intrusive all the time, is by now even stronger, and so I suppose that there might be bodies decomposing here and there, all around the place, if not in the village itself. And as we walk on, under the sky I've already described, I'm thinking my thoughts about the persons on either side of me, and finally about myself. On my left the supervisor, shorter than me but more talkative, and while walking he was dragging one leg and he would draw lines in the dust with his cane. An individual, as I now know, even more opaque and complex than I'd supposed in the "dining room." But then, I tell myself, it's pointless to try to imagine anyone, even the simplest of persons, as a rounded and complete and quite distinct being, because there are always rifts. Rifts which, it occurs to me, are like the creases in the supervisor's face.

Well now, he exclaims and wipes the sweat from his forehead, now it's my turn.

What do you mean, I ask.

I want to ask, he says, breathing heavily into my face, if you know who I am.

Well, I say, you're the supervisor here.

Anything more?

Not that I know.

That, he says, is not enough. Well, he says, so that you'll know it at last: I'm an unfortunate man.

An unfortunate man, I ask.

Yes, he says, an unfortunate man. Just look, for instance, how I'm sweating.

I look at him. Yes, I say, you're sweating. Then it occurs to me: I'm sweating, too, in which case I'm an unfortunate man as well.

No, he says, you sweat in a different way. You sweat in the healthy way, I sweat in the sick way. So, he says, after a short pause, let's not talk about my health.

You mean, I ask, it's not good?

So let's not talk about it, he says.

All right, I say.

And about my domestic circumstances, he says, a moment later, I'd better not tell you anything either. About the so-called family and its various members.

As you wish, I say.

Unless, of course, he says, you insist.

But I don't, I say.

Well, he says, I'm grateful to you for that. For I haven't known for years the thing they call the pleasures of the family. You understand?

Yes, I say, the pleasures of the family.

Good, he says, you've understood. You see, I have a wife, she's called Mariuccia. Of course, she's not so young anymore, but she's not old, either. And this wife . . . But what should I do, *dottore,* what should I do? Plainly I have to put up with it. You see, she's still quite pretty, you understand, especially her hair, her mouth. So that I'm not allowed to muss her hair and have to close my eyes and clench my teeth and, at certain times, I mustn't go home. And when I do go home, everything I see, everything I hear, everything I smell, I have to swallow it, as it were, with clenched teeth. Don't get me wrong, he exclaims, I've never caught them together. I'll have to be careful never to do that, he says. Before I come into the house, I whistle and make noises. On purpose, you understand, *dottore,* so they can hear I'm coming. Yes, *signor,* he exclaims, he visits my house, the *padrone* does, and we all celebrate Mariuccia's birthday together. We celebrate the birthdays of our five children together, too. And it's been going on for eleven years. That's to say, every Wednesday, when I'm out, evenings between six and eight. But sometimes also on other days and at other times, if not entirely regularly. He always sends me away. For instance, to Gibilmanna, to buy flower bulbs. As if, he says, you understand, as if I hadn't got anything inside my pants for my wife myself! Yes, he says, *i potenti.* Yet he does hold a protective hand over us, which isn't difficult, of course, considering his position. Not only over her, which is to be expected, but also over her children, yes, even over me. He's not out to destroy me, he's content with things the way they now are. So my job as supervisor, as long as he's alive and pays his Wednesday visits, is quite safe. Yet, believe me, *signor,* it's not easy. No pleasures of the family, he says, and shakes his head. Tell me what you think.

Well, I say, what could I tell you? You're quite right.

It's because of my honor, he says.

So it's your honor.

Yes, he says, no honor.

What you're saying only confirms what I thought, I say, the moment I got out of the car—we had a breakdown. That there are customs and practices hereabouts which, for people like us, you know . . .

There now, he exclaims, slapping his left thigh as he walks along, just see what a hard time I have! And here, see how the hairs are growing out of my nose, my ears! *È troppo,* he suddenly exclaims, in a loud voice. And so, you must realize, in the course of a human life, as soon as one gets older, as soon as one dares to get older, things build up. And one day there's a whole mountain, yes, a whole heap. First a little heap, but it keeps on growing and in time it becomes a bigger heap, and finally, when one's my age, a great big heap that you can't see around. And the whole heap always belongs to just one person. It's her heap, only hers, you must realize, and in my case my heap. Others have other heaps, everybody has one. Do you see, he asks, what I mean when I say that I'm an unfortunate man? And that I'd rather not talk about my own person, my own heap. But, well, I talk about anything and everything else, things that are not me. For instance, about our countryside, our history, our weather, about the lofty humanity of our classical age, or else about nature, even, or about the ornamentation of the balconies. And now, he says, what should I talk about now? About the ornamentation, lofty humanity, or nature? No, he exclaims, and straightens up somewhat, let's talk about our history. And he tells me, while undoing another shirt button, that in the second century on the island, where the salt mines now are, there was a lawmaker, who slept on beds made of ivory and had his racehorses groomed with combs of silver. And who had his secretaries catalog carefully all the grounds for the existence of God. That shows, he says, how God-fearing we've always been. Are you also a Christian or Protestant? He had them catalogued, I ask.

Yes, he says.

And were such grounds discovered, I ask.

Yes, he says, and immediately catalogued.

And what sort of grounds were they, I ask and hope for a moment there might be one that was valid *still today* and might really prove to me that there's a God, which might perhaps improve our situation, and not only here in D.

All documents about the cataloguing, he says, as well as those about the lawmaker, have been lost.

72

I look at him, contemplating for a while the uniform movement of his serious, weighty face. Then suddenly I laugh, I can't help it. Lost, I exclaim.

Si, signor, he says. Even the name of the lawmaker, he adds has been lost.

His name, too, I exclaim.

Si, signor, he says. Together with the other sights of the region.

Well, at least the tower is left, I say, because for quite a long time there has been no talk about the tower.

Si, signor, he says.

And what sort of a tower is it, if one may ask, I say, hoping that, after telling us so much about the Foundlings' Home, he'll tell us something about the tower, but I'm wrong.

Well, he simply says, the tower is my idea, is based on an idea of mine.

You built it, I ask.

No, he says, I didn't build it.

So what do you mean when you say it's based on an idea of yours?

The tower, he says, and after outlining it in the air rapidly with a weighty hand he pushes it resolutely out of our way, you'll never be able to understand it on your own, but we'll understand it, all of us together, in about an hour, when we'll be sitting in front of it, stretching our legs, in the comfortable armchairs.

So one can sit down by the tower, I ask.

Yes, he says, one can sit.

So there are armchairs by the tower, I ask.

Yes, he says, there are chairs.

Aha, I say, and reflect that great hopes must hang from the tower, if there are chairs around it. So have they been, I ask, put around the tower.

Yes, he says, that's right.

So that one can stretch one's legs?

Yes, he says, that too is possible.

Did you hear that, Maria, at the tower one can sit, I say to my wife. At last you'll be able to stretch your legs. Just think, we'll be there any moment.

Yes, indeed, the supervisor says, your husband is quite right.

And the spectacle, I ask.

The spectacle starts, he says, when we're all seated. In an hour, as I said. Yes, the spectacle starts in about an hour. And the look in his eye tells me he has no more to say on the subject.

Listen, I say, one more question, while we're talking about it. For some reason that I don't know myself, I simply can't stop thinking about your tower. And it occurred to me, just when you were talking about the chairs, that I might perhaps already know the tower. That I've seen this tower before, even if it was long ago, yes, it's so long ago that, as I always say, it's just not true. That your tower, just imagine, might perhaps be the tower I saw about twenty years ago, together with a young Italian friend. You see, I can remember a tower. I remember that I walked around a tower with him, arm in arm, in a southern countryside—but where was it?—several times, and it was very hot. A romanesque building from Norman times, something bulky, firm, round. Does your tower date from Norman times?

What? he asks.

Yes, I say, firm and round.

Well, I can't tell you exactly when the tower dates back to, the supervisor says, and he stops walking for a moment, but it's certainly round. Then he walks on and has forgotten the tower. In any case, he speaks no more of it, but of something quite different: a British sailing ship, the frigate *Amalia*, which in 1831 discovered an island, just off the coast, till then unknown, shaped like a teardrop, not marked on any ocean map, a nameless and stateless place which, as a hastily prepared expedition to the island found out, had only risen out of the sea a few days earlier, and concerning which there had been at once, naturally, a diplomatic dispute between the Bourbon and British governments, as to who owned it. The conflict had still not been settled when the island, with a gurgle, sank into the sea, just as it had risen out of it.

Sank! I exclaim and start to laugh. Did you hear that, Maria, it sank again. Sank! I exclaim again.

Si, signor, he says, earnestly.

Well, I say, and everything I have about me, my cameras, the money in my pockets, is rattling with my laughter, that's a nice story! The island that came and went. Something to smile about. Don't you think so, Maria, I say.

But my wife doesn't smile, she remains quite unmoved, and she says nothing.

Well, I say, even if she won't admit it, she likes it. Vanished! Vanished! I exclaim.

Yes, indeed. And one fine day, not so distant, this bigger island too, the one we're on, together with all the other islands, will vanish into the sea again, he exclaims and waves his cane.

You think so, I say, but how?

Well, he says, either in the natural way. Everyone knows the region is volcanic.

Or, I ask.

Or in the other way, he says, and places his paw on his sexual organ. There had been quite an interval since the last war.

You think so, I ask.

Yes, I do, he says.

So much for the supervisor, who sweats a lot on Wednesdays, toward evening, and not only because of the heat. On the other side of me my wife, who has other problems. Because of her flimsy shoes—I had warned her—she has the greatest difficulties with the dusty, stony, potholed earth underfoot. I keep on having to prop her up, if not lift her. Suddenly, on this walk of ours to the tower, in this disease-ridden, filthy, flyblown, rat-scuffling place, she wants to know whether I still love her.

Whether I . . . , I ask.

Yes, she says.

Well, I say, stopping for a moment, to catch my breath for the necessary answer and to let the supervisor, who shouldn't hear the answer, walk a few steps ahead. Well, I

76

say, deciding to be quite cool and obliging. And while the drops of sweat are leaping out of my hair like small warm liquid animals: Look now, I say, just look now! And I point to the supervisor walking ahead, and I say: Sh! Not in front of him. And then I point to the sky and exclaim: The sun, for Chrisake! And then to her, quietly: That under such circumstances and in such surroundings and with such worries on my mind, for which I have you to thank, *another child,* I exclaim. Under such circumstances, I say, it was impossible to answer the question. As if everything hadn't been agreed and settled. And that I supposed her mother, who's had an easy time of it and had only one child herself, to be behind this break in our agreement. You needn't shake your head like that, I say. She's all for a second child, of course, because she doesn't have to feed it and bring it up. And I finish my reply with words to the effect that, under such circumstances, the question whether I still loved her was altogether inept.

So you don't love me anymore, she says, brushing the dust from her skirt as she walks along.

I make a dismissive gesture. I shake my head. No, I say, it's not that. And I sign to her that this inference is much too hasty, much too empty-headed. Because really things are not that way. Because my physical needs and concerns, I explain to her, in words to that effect—fear, worry, heat, thirst, also the exertion of walking—had at present set aside and killed all possible feelings I might have, and that I'd rather not say anything about what had been temporarily killed off and set aside.

So you've killed me off, she says.
There you go, misunderstanding me again, I exclaim.
So what you've done is set me aside, she says.
It may seem like that to you, perhaps, I say, but . . . Quiet,
I say, not now, the supervisor.

8

Who now stops and lets us catch up with him, walking
through the hot, shimmering air. For we've reached the
marketplace, *il mercato*. And now we're walking across it,
without realizing that it's the marketplace. We're thinking,
aha, a piazza again, a meadow, a ruined field, whereas
we're actually, just think, in the *mercato*. So the supervisor tells us, as he stops, groaning with the heat. The
supervisor, sweat streaming from his forehead, through
his hair. Thus the supervisor enlightens us. He tells us
we're in the marketplace.
Aha, we exclaim, stopping and looking around, aha.
And it's a sad thing, he continues, that the marketplace in
D. is nowadays so depopulated and vacant and no longer
exists at all as a market with merchants, booths, *affari*, he
exclaims, *affari*. Rather, what we have before us is a broad,
barren expanse with a few fir trees and cypresses at its
edges, which might have once given the square a solemn,
even sublime look, but which now stand around with
tattered outlines, looking sort of scorched. And on the

earth, naturally, excrement drying in the sun. At the upper end of the marketplace, beyond the trees, broad-fronted and distant, the façade of a courthouse, once imposing and dominant with its baroque splendor, but now devastated by age, shaken by earthquakes, dismantled from within. Shuffling closer to it we see from its window openings— without glass, like scoured eye sockets goggling at us—that, like the Foundlings' Home, it is empty.

Well, says the supervisor, who really is somewhat embarrassed by the condition of his marketplace—as if he'd only noticed it in our presence—well, he says, I hope you're not disappointed with our marketplace.

Not knowing what to say, I simply spread my arms, with the purse, with the cameras.

But, for the time being, he says, don't dismiss it, before it has been explained to you. Because it's not admittedly a question of some contemporary and folklorist phenomenon, to be seen and touched, rather of something, so to speak, faded from history, which, even if it was invisible still, well, really, the spirit of the place . . .

What do you mean, I ask, and scrape my shoes in the dust. I mean, on the one hand there's the place, he says, and on the other there's time.

What, I ask, still entangled deep down in my wife's question, what are you talking about?

Quite right, he says. Certainly the *mercato* was no longer visible, not everything could be visible, but nevertheless we were standing on the spot where it had been visible once.

You mean? I ask the supervisor.

Here, he exclaims, and stamps both feet.

Aha, I exclaim, aha.

In earlier times, he goes on, amongst other things, the market of D. had been here. True, the peasants no longer came, and no customers either, and this spot in the universe was now, so to speak, empty. Everything's empty, he says, except what people hereabouts have in their heads. So that here, in spite of the emptiness, even though as visitors we couldn't know it—here was a historic site, the most historic site of all.

Confronted with the rack and ruin of the whole area, incredulous, also impatient, also because I have the impression that he's leading us by the nose, and because I want finally, finally to get to the tower, I simply say Aha, aha. For one thing's obvious to me: This place called D., in all its misery, has nothing, absolutely nothing to show us. And I hold my wife back by the arm and am wanting to resume our conversation, when she says: You never did love me.

I never . . . , I say.

No, she says, you never did love me.

Please, Maria, I say, don't let's talk of it now. Let's save it for later, then we'll talk it over. And I promise her: When we're back home again and the danger of the child is past and she's got over it all—if it weren't quite safe I wouldn't be giving you such advice and asking you to get rid of the thing—then, I say, then we'll have time again for my feelings about you, and for yours about me. As for mine, they haven't changed in years. Not until now, I say. Yet perhaps we needn't be worried, I say, perhaps you're wrong and there's no child on the way. And if it is, it can still—what with the strain or the heat, or walking and jumping and climbing, and who knows, I say, perhaps we can even climb up the tower—then, you realize, it can still put itself spontaneously right. Don't you think? I ask. And encourage her, something I probably shouldn't have done, because it could be misunderstood, and in her condition she misunderstands everything, to help this spontaneity out with a few energetic movements, little leaps perhaps, I say. Yes, I exclaim, or whisper, or think, such leaps could help. Look, I exclaim. And point to the trackless ground and the stones that we're walking over and which the supervisor, who's walking on ahead of us, but— I can see—is hearing everything and seeing everything and is about to come closer again and meddle in our conversation, calls our eternal primeval rock.

Stop coming so close to us, I exclaim, and stretch an arm out. Keep your distance.

What do you mean by *close*, he exclaims, and why distance? Excuse me, of course, distance. But that's difficult, he says, if one has to do one's professional work and explain things.

Explain, I exclaim, what is there to explain now?

The *mercato*, he says, the *mercato*.

Then explain, I say, but be quick about it.

Well then, on the marketplace, the supervisor tells us, explains to us, as we walk on, all popular insurrections and revolutions had begun and ended, up into the nineteenth century. Whatever kind of insurrection or revolution it may have been, whatever sort of attempt to change things, this was the place where it ended, here, he says,

and makes a semicircle with his cane. For we must surely
have been asking ourselves: Under the conditions that
existed here, and still do exist, had there been no insurrection, no revolution, no attempt to change things? For
the conditions, and of course we were right about them,
were unbearable. What can a person live off, he exclaims
with a sudden vehemence, in a country where the soil
yields nothing, and the factory promised by the govern-
ment doesn't arrive? As for the testimonies of the past,
without an occasional sight of which affluent visitors think
their lives wasted, none could be found. So that any paid
work, even the humblest, could only be arrived at by having connections and contacts, or through bribery. To become supervisor here, he exclaims, pointing to his sash,
even that was only possible if one wasn't at home at the
crucial moment. Yet one can't be choosy, there's too much
misery, too many people without work, if one person
doesn't do it, another will. This had always been so in D.,
and it always would be so. Yet even here there had been
insurrections and revolutions, except that none had been
successful. And he talks about this, while tracing figures in
the dust with his cane, figures I've by now come to recognize, little men with heads, bodies, and limbs, which he
scratches out the moment he has traced them. Well, he
tells us, even in D. there had been brave and dauntless and
resolute men, who, as a sign of protest, had cut their hair
short and revolted against the conditions of life, oh yes.
And if we were to ask him what he thought of these men,
he'd say he took his hat off to them. And indeed, as he
ambles onward, he removes his round cap and renders

homage to them though fleetingly, in spirit, with a bow. Men, he goes on, having put his cap back on again—after quickly wiping it clean—men whom the people itself had brought forth and held aloft for a few days and then forsaken and betrayed, and, here in the marketplace, which was also at one time architecturally unique, also, well, torn to pieces.

Architecturally unique, I ask, so was there something here once?

Lots, he exclaims, lots. Palaces, gardens, fountains, columns. Everything, he exclaims, everything. Only today one couldn't see it anymore, unfortunately. And so many heroes—he couldn't enumerate them all to us in the short time left before the spectacle.

At the tower, I say, interrupting him.

Yes, at the tower, he says, for we'll be there in a moment. And he treads more firmly on his way. Well: in the time left before we reach the tower . . . But now I'm no longer listening to him, but thinking, having once more rapidly given a thought to the tower, about my wife. And I'm thinking—except that this hope isn't voiced—ah, if only she'd trip over, if only she'd trip over, trip over! If only she'd hurt herself, just the tiniest bit, because if she'd stumble, just a little, she'd have a spontaneous miscarriage that would save me, of course, much trouble, care, and anxiety. Look, I tell her, letting the supervisor carry on talking, I just don't listen to him, and I show her how she could walk so as to make a jump, so that, who knows, perhaps the whole thing would spontaneously be settled. Look, I exclaim, look! And I take a firm hold of her and, my legs being naturally much longer and stronger, suddenly take a long stride, almost a jump, and I pull her and drag her and haul her along with me. Since she hadn't anticipated the leap, she shrieks, flounders, and she does fall, but only gently, not dangerously, and I pull her at once upright again.

She extracts her arm from my grip, takes her arm away from me, so to speak, and rests it against her forehead, saying: So you want to kill me now?

Kill? Me? My own wife? One more reproach, a novel one, this time. I strike a posture, as if uncomprehending.

So you want to kill me now? she exclaims, a second time.

Or should I kill myself for you?

Should you what?

Wouldn't that be the easiest way, she asks.

Ridiculous! Ridiculous, of course. A wicked thought, even an evil thought. Yet I exonerate myself. I even lay my hand on my heart. I hadn't wanted her to stumble. And anyway, I say, it wasn't so bad. But now she's begun to cry. How embarrassing, and not only for me. How embarrassing for the supervisor, who's walking ahead, acting, to be sure, as if he hadn't seen her stumble, and doesn't want to see her tears, either! Yet I'm certain that nothing escapes him, that he hears, sees, perceives everything. And my own discomfiture, although nothing has happened. It's nothing, I exclaim, nothing happened! And what I'm thinking is that now and again one has to be somewhat ruthless, also with regard to oneself, but I don't say that, I say nothing and let the supervisor have the field, do the talking, do the explaining.

Well then, in the time before we'd reach the tower he couldn't possibly tell us about all the dauntless men whom his people had brought forth and torn to pieces on this marketplace, there were simply too many of them. So only the highlights, and those briefly. All right: for example, the unforgotten executions of 1799 that had gone on for months. This happened when a few benefactors and utopians had thought that they, too, should declare a republic and bring *freedom* to the people. Freedom! he exclaims, and bursts into a laugh, waving his cane in the air. And what did the people do with freedom? Well, they didn't do the slightest thing with it, but after a few days changed sides and went back to the old tyrants. They betrayed the freedom fighters, took them out of their beds at night and executed them, mostly still in their nightshirts, here on the marketplace. That's why you should take a good look at the marketplace, he exclaims. Anyone who wore his hair short, in the latest fashion, had simply been . . . And he draws a finger across his throat.

Beheaded, I ask.

First hanged, he exclaims, then drawn and quartered. Over there, he says, and points in the direction of the courthouse, past which at this moment two women dressed in black are walking, the first we've seen in D., with plastic pails on their heads—we don't know who they are or what the pails contain, we don't know anything at all—over there had stood the gallows, sometimes as many as seven. Yes, he exclaims, all this is traditional knowledge, all established fact. And to that place—he points to the courthouse—the people of D., who didn't want any freedom at all, had taken in an old wheelcart their liberators, who appealed to their reason up till the last moment, in vain. First they dragged the liberators to the scaffold, then to the ladders, where the hangmen, noose in hand, were waiting for them. Since, for one thing, there had been very many people with short hair, whether or not for political reasons, and, for another, many people had had no occupation to pursue, and since haste had been necessary, because right after the daily executions the daily winning lottery numbers were drawn, the people had created the office of the Foot Pullers, the *tirapiedi*; these were the ones who, when the liberators were already strung up and the hangmen were pressing down on their shoulders, had to take hold of their feet so as to quicken the procedure—the lottery! the lottery!— and pull. He could assure us that this office, which re- quired no previous training, had for a long time been one of the most sought-after in D.

Don't you realize, I say, that what you're telling us . . .

It interests you? he asks, delighted.

Well, I say, and am about to say that, for our taste, he's going too far, much too far. Also that his account is far too precise, with too many details. Do we, as tourists, have no right to a touristic relationship with the market of D.? Can't we, as visitors, be allowed here, as elsewhere, to stop at the surface of things? But I don't ask these questions. I ask: And where's your tower?

The tower, he says and looks down between his feet, is another matter.

And where is it, I ask.

The tower, he says, comes after the market, which comes after the Foundlings' Home.

All right, I say, let's walk on. You go ahead, so we're not treading on one another's heels.

And as soon as the supervisor, whom I even have to *push* away from us, in front of us, is finally walking ahead of us again and we can see his broad sweating back, I quietly ask my wife: Well, how do you feel now?

The same, she says.

So you've still got problems? I mean, hasn't anything changed? I ask.

No.

And you're still feeling sick?

Yes.

Well, I say, wiping both arms, first the right, then the left, across my steaming forehead, the exertion, you know, the physical thing, might have started it moving.

And she, looking me in the eye as she walks along, full of hatred, full of disgust: You swine, she says, you swine.

All right now, the supervisor says, and he stops again. Probably he has ideas—because we'd like, he supposes, always to be hearing something from him, seeing something too. So now he invents the *ladder*. Well now, the ladder, he says, while brushing his left thumb down his cheek. And he takes us to a fence, against which a ladder is propped, a quite ordinary ladder. *Coincidence*, I tell myself at first, but soon I'm convinced that the ladder has been propped against the fence on purpose, perhaps he put it there himself, *for us*.

88

Please take a look at this ladder, he exclaims and steps aside.

Yes, yes, I say, we know: a ladder, I say, and glance at it.

But then the supervisor shouts No! and stamps both feet. It was no ordinary ladder. It was the ladder up which the heroes had climbed to the gallows.

Up this ladder, I exclaim. I was already walking on. Yes, indeed, he says, up this ladder. And now take hold of it, take hold of the ladder.

Why, I ask.

To take hold of the historic ladder, he exclaims, is permitted. So, go ahead.

All right, I say, if you insist. We'll take hold of it. Come on, Maria, I say, take hold of the ladder.

Yes, he says, do, it's not prohibited.

All right, I'm thinking, and I take a few steps forward. Now then, I say. I stand by the ladder and stoop and actually do take hold—my wife refuses to do so—of the ladder that's propped against the fence—what a farce, I'm thinking. That's how it was: on this Wednesday afternoon, walking through this village, in which we've been, so to speak, left hanging in midair, because our car broke down, something wrong with the transmission, as I later hear, and which, after the ladder, at the very latest when, at a certain moment, the supervisor stoops over a dead rat and picks it up by the tail, brandishing it under our noses, we should have left, an impossible and ghastly place. Then at least we'd have avoided the tower and the events around it, yet we had no idea what these events would be, we couldn't possibly know. So that I keep on telling myself:

No, don't turn back. Because first you must see the tower, even if you don't know why. Thus, on this afternoon, on our tour of the place, the swine walking between the others thinks quickly one more time about his tower and he exploits, once the supervisor has thrown away the rat with an apology—*un piccolo giuoco,* he exclaims—and has wiped his hand on his trousers, the momentary awkward pause to set his arguments against the child distinctly in order. Yes, the swine reflects and closes his eyes, those arguments—he counts them, there are six—you must organize them now quickly in your swinish head. And this very evening, right after the tower, you'll recite them to her. Or, at the very latest, tonight, when you take hold of her from behind and hold her tight in bed—it's wide, but not high off the floor—you'll speak into her ear your six arguments from behind. Because if she waits any longer it'll be too late to intervene.

9

□ □
□

Our arrival at the tower, me in the middle, my wife behind me, the supervisor, although it's almost evening, with sweat streaming down his forehead, but his back and armpits are sweaty too, for it's a mistake to think one sweats on this island only at midday, it's just not so. As we arrive at the tower, keeping step, the supervisor, gasping, continues to walk three or four paces ahead, on his short legs, although the impediment with which he walks and which I noticed when he first appeared, has got worse, and his left leg is dragging over the ground, scratching a trail. So then: as we arrive at the tower—suddenly it's there in front of us—I see at once that my hopes and expectations for it are not to be realized. It's not the tower around which I walked, before my marriage, with a friend, quite the contrary: it's not old, high, noble, as I had imagined, nor is it bulky and round; the longed-for tower, the dreaded tower fails to keep its promise. It could be any-where and it's perfectly ordinary. I'll be describing it as it looms up before us in the pink evening light, as we emerge with a sigh of relief, our feet swollen and sore, from the village of D., arriving in an open area between the access to the village and a grove of cypress trees—which turned out to be the cemetery. Briefly: a water tower. Not ancient, not a monument, but an eyesore, nineteenth century. And the flags, the imagined flags? No flags, either. Yet in the time of our great-grandfathers such towers were raised now and then in the arid and flat regions of our continent, where the terrain made reservoirs unfeasible; a cistern served to store the water, and in the chamber at the base of the tower there'd be the switches and pipes for the regulation of the water pressure. Later, the pipes and switches ceased to function, on account of their age, but these towers, their survival assured by the durability of the building materials and by the mindlessness of authorities always far away, were simply forgotten and were left standing in the countryside. And so, on the pretext of showing us a sight worth seeing, the supervisor has brought us to just such a tower, obsolete, forgotten, and still standing, because in D. there's nothing else to be seen. And now, his wide open mouth shimmering with gold-capped teeth, he's expecting us to thank him for his trouble and offer a word in recognition of this tower, which is especially damaged and battered around the entrance and is obviously disintegrating inside also, but no such word occurs to me. With my legs apart I stand there, ferns reaching to my knees, the purse with the money on my wrist, and look the tower up and down. What a disappointment! How can you have been so crazy, I tell myself, listening to him and letting him drag you here. He's not a supervisor, he's a *furbo.* And how naive you were, all the fancies you had about the tower! What am I to say to him now? That the tower is beautiful? Ridiculous. Old? No, it's not old. High? Well, seven or eight meters perhaps, but it's easy to imagine a higher tower. The only thing about it that stares one in the face is its being utterly useless and superfluous, but can I say so? Best say nothing at all, perhaps I'll think of something later. Hands clasped behind me, I walk up and down in front of the tower a few times and say: One thing's for sure, Herr Hans, you'd have done well to put a lighter coat on this morning.

Yes, the supervisor says, fanning himself with his home-made handkerchief, you're probably right about that.

This coat you're wearing, I say, and point to it, isn't suitable for this climate. It's much too heavy. You've sweated all the way through it.

As if I didn't know, he says, and to show me he's aware of it he raises his arms, so that I see the sweat marks. Unfortunately, he says, he owns no other dark coat less heavy than this one.

Does it have to be dark, I ask, and am glad that he's so easily distracted from his tower.

Yes, he says, it has to be dark.

Yes, but aren't dark clothes here, I ask, just a convention that should have been abolished long ago, considering the climate? A black coat in this heat?

Yes, yes, he says, it has to be dark.

Unnecessary, unnecessary, I exclaim and wipe his dark coat away with a single gesture. Take a tip from me, just wear a shirt, I exclaim and I swivel once around, so that

93

he can see me from all sides. I don't wear a coat, but for this place, this *Kaff*, I even say, it's enough. And since I have the impression that he doesn't understand the word *Kaff*, I explain what it means, successfully, I think. But because I don't want to offend him, having for some time had the impression that he's very touchy inside his thick skull, I quickly add that when I'm at home I run around in just a shirt, even in the smaller places, where, as anyone knows, there are the nicest people, without embarrassment to myself or others. No offense meant, I say. And your German, I exclaim, is excellent. And that my suggestion implies nothing against him or his country, quite the contrary. In a shirt, in a shirt, I exclaim and once more make a show of my white holiday shirt, though it too is sticking to my skin and chest and has great rings of sweat under the arms.

In a shirt, the supervisor says, that's impossible. And quietly, having contemplated my shirt for a while, he shakes his head. I cannot walk about in just a shirt today, he says. I even have to wear a necktie, he says, and points to it. And then, with some annoyance, because it finally occurs to him that he has allowed me to distract him from his beloved tower and to involve him in a conversation about shirts and trousers, he says: Well, what do you say? And he points to the top of the tower with his cane, holding it like a rapier.

So he hasn't been distracted after all, I'm thinking. Now you've got to say something about the tower. Ah yes, is all I say, there's your tower.

Correct, the supervisor says, and through the ferns he

walks, making a broad track, stumping closer to the tower, and then, like me on the *dammuso*, knocking on it with his fist a few times.

Terrific, I say and yawn.

Isn't it, he says.

Amazing, I say.

Yes, he says, yes indeed.

An old water tower, isn't it, I suddenly say, so that he'll know I recognize what it is. And, because I don't want to offend him, I too walk up to the tower, make as if to knock on it with my fist, but, out of exaggerated respect, I merely scratch on it a little with my fingers.

Yes, the supervisor says, a water tower. That too, he says, that too. And what was my impression. And he wants me to describe my impression, quite candidly, *holding nothing back*. And he looks at me from the side, as I can see out of the corner of an eye, so as to read the impression from my face.

And me, letting a little time pass and still having no idea what to say about the tower: Well, I say, and I take up my stance before the tower, my hands thrust as deeply as possible into my pockets, with a slight smile—It's just a tower, isn't it?

Then the supervisor, and there's no way I can stop him, suddenly falls into raptures, speaks of a magnificent building, which would have suited him perfectly, forgets who is standing before him, who beside him, continues in Sicilian, lays first his cane, then his hand, then almost his head on my shoulder, and, believing that I share his emotion, is on the verge of embracing me then and there in front of the tower. I keep pushing him away, but he keeps coming back. Easy now, Herr Hans, I say, and pat his hand, easy now.

What's that?

Yes, yes, I say, it's all right.

Questions, he then exclaims, I should question him. Had I any questions?

Questions? What about? No wonder that with all his display of zeal I can hardly bite back a smile. No, I exclaim, no questions.

No questions? he asks, disappointedly.

No.

For since we're so close to his tower, have even touched his tower, I can dispense with all questions about the tower. Because the tower itself shows us what it stands on, what it is made of. Of the dark volcanic stone of the region, lumps big as fists, with coarse mortar between them, which, in many places, as if fingers had been pushed through it, has crumbled away. Many stones are missing from the tower, even whole layers and levels. It's held together by itself, I'm thinking. And its outer skin of stone, exposed to all weathers, is encrusted with moss and lichen. Thus the tower simultaneously collapses and grows out of the tall ferns. And then, after we've made a thorough inspection of the foot of the tower, after we've touched it, even knocked on it, and after we've once more walked, no, been dragged around it—*venga! venga!*—the supervisor tugs a rusty key from his trouser pocket and means to go into the tower. Into it? Yes, into it. And why? To climb it, climb it, he exclaims. Naturally we refuse. We

96

exclaim: Climb it, why? And shake our heads. And wave his suggestion away, from our position in the ferns, with determined gestures. My wife, having gloomy thoughts, even stamps her feet. As if we hadn't got viewing towers like this where we live too. And we remind the supervisor, who's been leading us around his tower open-mouthed for much too long already, of his promise to consider our exhaustion and spare us all strains, all crawling and climbing. For his tower, though ugly, is high. Never before have I seen, let alone climbed, a tower at once so high and so ugly. Now I'm estimating its height to be eight or nine meters, if not more, as I look up, my head tilted back on my shoulders. And my wife, in her condition! I look at her. She's pale. Perhaps . . . But no, she shakes her head. Her condition is unchanged. A condition which might, I'm thinking, be altered by the unforeseen exertion of climbing a tower, by certain motions of the legs and torso. Granted she really is pregnant, granted it's not an illusion. And I'm thinking once more the same thoughts as on our walk through D. this afternoon, only worse. For when I now think: she might stumble, I'm thinking: Ah, if only she'd stumble. And when I think: In the darkness she might fall, I'm thinking: Ah, if only she'd fall. I, the more exhausted of us two, with the heavy cameras, with, when it comes to climbing, at the mere thought of climbing, my slight heart problem, the sweats I break into, my shortness of breath—I wipe my forehead with a handkerchief. When it comes to sweating, I'm like the supervisor. It also occurs to me that I've always detested high buildings, have avoided living in them, climbing them, as far as possible.

THE SPECTACLE AT THE TOWER

I can't even lean out of the window of my third-floor office, not even lean over the solidly secure balcony of my home on the Moritzstrasse, without feeling dizzy, without feeling that I'm falling, already in midair. So should I climb this tower that has been unrelentingly talked into the middle of my life, this tower which, as it turns out, is a deception and leaves me completely cold? Ridiculous, I'm thinking. And I exclaim: Ridiculous! Or at least: Impossible, much too high, I exclaim. But the supervisor has already taken a grip on his cane and is pointing to the tower with it, and he draws his cane, as far as it will reach, several times across the tower's base, making an altogether peculiar sound, a clattering, also a scratching. And he exclaims: Certainly, yes! Climb it! Climb it! Listen, Herr Hans, I exclaim, and I plant my feet firmly on the ground. And I'm about to lay my hand on his shoulder, with a confiding gesture I've learned from observing him, but I withdraw my hand just in time. And I ask him to realize that, by accompanying him through D., from one end to the other, we've already responded to him generously, so that it was now quite unnecessary for us to climb the tower. Yet the idea of having any obligation toward us obviously doesn't penetrate the supervisory skull. For, without our being able to stop him, he has already thrust the tower key into the tower lock and he's opening the tower door, then he pushes the door open, it yields with a squeak, and he exclaims that, for any understanding of the spectacle, it is imperative that we should climb the tower. Why? So that we can see how high it is. High? Can't we see quite well enough how high it is,

98

his tower? Haven't we been resolutely staring up at it, our heads tilted back on our shoulders? Yes, he says, but only when you're *at the top* can you really see it. See what? The height. At the top? Yes.

All right then, I'm thinking, all right! And reluctantly, after making a sign to my wife meaning *We'll climb it,* I yield to the beckoning of the supervisor—what a title!— and we pass through the iron door, with its rust-eaten corners, into the tower's interior structure, its murky spiral stairwell. And of course we walk into the most dense and disgusting stench. My God, how foul the interiors of such old towers are! In which generations of people have relieved themselves, in small and large ways. We walk on corpses too, me on something furry, soft, my poor wife on something hard. That's to say, I tread, as is revealed in the dull light, on the remains of a rat, she on the gnawed, stripped and dried skeleton of a feathered creature. A raven, we're thinking, or a crow, which was lying here when the rat came in to make a meal of it. And we turn this way and that in our walking shoes, in the darkness, not knowing what to think. We can't see whatever else might be lying in the corners. And so we climb, leaving the hard and the soft behind us, upward, groping our way, having already walked around the tower outside, now around the inside, in semidarkness, arms outstretched, turning and climbing incessantly around one another as we tap with our hands and shuffle our feet and gasp at the air. No, we had no idea this tower is so high! And at each turn of its flat smooth stairs we see through an air vent an earth newly transformed farther and farther beneath. No, we'd had no idea this tower is so high. In front of us the supervisor climbs, knowing his way, every so often giving explanations which we don't understand, because the tower has such an echo. (Also the footsteps of the supervisor, who in the uncertain light, when he looks back over his shoulder, now has skin the color of a regular corpse, echo, the scraping and scratching of his feet, his gasping, his cane tapping.) Behind him my wife climbs, she keeps stopping, sighing all the time, all the time worried about her shoes, always groping for a hold or a support, all the time wringing her hands. I, last, follow her, drive her onward, with small cries of encouragement, also with hisses, but I too have to keep stopping and supporting myself, so that the ascent of the tower, which I'd like to have done with as soon as possible, is quite unnecessarily prolonged. Good, just a bit farther. Good, we're at the top. Through a hatchway, through which, the supervisor exclaims, nobody has climbed all spring and summer, and which he now pushes open, we emerge into the open air. And now at the top of the tower we're wondering what we're supposed to do in the open air. Swallows are whizzing around our heads, the fair weather sky is close. And all around us, once we've stood up straight into the sky and our eyes have accustomed themselves to its light, a positively measureless, arid landscape, coppery in the last rays of the sun that's sinking into the sea, a landscape with shrubs, bushes, a hill here and there, also mountains, mainly bare. Evidently the edge of the world, the limit at which everything stops. And away over this limit, from outside, over the sea, the hot wind blows in our faces when we raise them. Cautiously, taking small steps, I shuffle to the guard wall. It hardly comes up to my knees. But there's a railing. I grip it at once and grope my way, gasping and groaning, the solid world far below me, toward the supervisor, who has gone ahead. For a while we stand together, speechless, deep in contemplation of the country beneath us. Steeply tilted at our feet the roofs of D., broken, jumbled, badly built. Chimneys have collapsed, there's black smoke, a vertical plume, over one of them, until a breeze comes and blows it that way and this. In between, small airless courtyards, now and then a gap, a hole, where something might once perhaps have been, but where there's nothing now. Farther off, when we raise our eyes, the country unfolds. Southward a mountain range unknown to me, in a misty glow. A bit of a river, which becomes visible when we twist our heads around. Then the maquis, in troughs and hollows, blank undulations, dells and humps, partly with dense and brown vegetation, partly spacious and touched with green. And behind the maquis, in the distance, as far as the eye can see, like liquid lead freshly poured, smooth and sunlit and unexcited: *il mare africano*, the African sea. Vertigo, to be so high above the world, so close to the tops of the cypress trees that one can see with a glance deep into their branches. Hands on the railing, cameras on my belly, I grope my way once around the platform and am careful not to look straight down. Rather, I look at my hands. And the landscape. Something to be seen, but once is enough. Meanwhile the supervisor points with his outstretched arm toward dark, cankerous sores on the bark of the cypress trees, rust brown discoloration of the branches, probably caused by a still undetermined disease. That's where they begin to die, he says. But we're too weak to look at the trees or to talk or even to listen; we're on the verge of exhaustion. How did we like the tower? We nod, speechless. The view? We wave him away. And the height of it, did we . . . ? What? How high the tower is, the supervisor exclaims, and he points to the sky. Yes, we say, and we look toward the hatchway. Only once, when he's turning the other way, do I look down into the depths below me. And, obeying an impulse out of my confused and desolate postwar childhood, a childhood meanwhile thrust aside and put behind me, I spat over the edge to the ground, onto the paving around the tower. And followed with my eyes for a very long, very long time the drop of spit as it fell through the air, to burst and scatter in a thousand million splashes on the stones below.

10

□ □

□

It turns out that close to the tower of D., located in the
cemetery, on the side opposite the tower door, there's a
flat, single-story, stone building that we'd overlooked, and
to which the supervisor, after we've descended the stair
without falling and have emerged again in the open air,
points our attention with his outstretched arm. He says
it's a café. A café? Yes, a café. Indeed it is one of the best,
he starts to boast, if not *the very best* café in . . .
In D., I ask.
No, he says, in the entire island.
In all Sicily, I exclaim and look at him incredulously.
Yes, indeed, he exclaims, and he gazes at it.
Well now, we're thinking, the best or not, a café on the
outskirts of a place is nothing unusual, and we stamp our
feet a few times, to feel solid ground under them. Yes, he
says, rubbing his hands, and moreover this café—something we couldn't yet have known—will be catering for
the spectacle. Ah, we say, and put our hands to our heads,
heavens, yes, the spectacle, of course! We'd almost entirely

forgotten about it, thinking so much about the tower and then climbing to the top of it. We thought there was nothing more to come, after the ascent of the tower. But this is evidently not the case, for if the tower is now behind us, the spectacle, as the supervisor assures us, still lies before us, and will at any moment begin, inside or outside this café. I give the supervisor a nudge. I say: Listen now, and I wink at him. And ask him if we couldn't—now that we've seen the tower, even climbed it—skip the spectacle or at least be absolved from it. A question I shouldn't have asked.

Skip the spectacle, he exclaims and he stops and goggles at me incredulously.

Scusi, if it's any trouble, I say, I was only asking.

We'd better forget that question right away, he says. And he spits in front of his feet. Right, he exclaims, in front of this café will very soon commence the spectacle, which can't be postponed or skipped.

Very well, I say, if you think so.

And now he's going to take us to this café, as his guests. Having closed the tower door behind us—unnecessary, for the very stench of it is enough to keep anyone out—he drags his feet before us across the tower area and toward the café. He, too, seems exhausted. If only he didn't limp so, how painful, I'm thinking. For instead of hobbling slightly as before, he now limps. And the handkerchief with which he keeps wiping his forehead is so wet that he can't put it back into his pocket anymore. About halfway between tower and café we have an encounter. The children are here again. The children? Yes, the goat-butchers, who had vanished from our thoughts. But we can't fail to recognize them in the evening light, by their arms and legs, which are still bloody from the butchering. Suddenly they're leaping out from behind the hedge that surrounds the cemetery, and they stand in our path. We notice particularly the one with the scar who knifed the goat and who now, with an earnest look and not saying a word, takes a few steps toward the supervisor. Wait a moment, I say to my wife and hold her back, for I don't want to be drawn into what might now happen. Because when, like us, one is in a country where one doesn't know either the customs or the language properly, one has to be careful, for one never knows. Yet my fears are superfluous. With a jest on his lips, the supervisor limps—arms outstretched, the way we know him—toward the boy, and he lays a slack red paw on the boy's skinny shoulder. And after patting him as one might pat a horse, he takes him by the nape and leads him toward us. This is Mario Diagonale, a good boy, a dauntless boy. We call him Mimiddu, he exclaims, pushing the boy along before him.

Buon giorno, Mimiddu, I say and hold my hand out to the boy, who keeps his head bowed.

Presto, il signore ti dice buon giorno, dai la mano, presto, exclaims the supervisor, but the boy, instead of extending a hand, slips both hands, which are trembling slightly, with a lovely gesture of refusal into his pockets. Let him be, I say, perhaps he's afraid of us.

Yes, but he needn't be, the supervisor says, I'm with him.

Let him be, I say, perhaps he's shy.

Possibly he's shy, the supervisor says. And excited, too,

because he has a difficult task before him, isn't that so, Mimiddu? he asks. And tugs at his hair gently, by way of punishing him for his disobedience. Did you see how curiously pale he is? Almost transparent, he says, and he lays his hand on the boy's cheek. Even his neck is pale, but the pallor suits him. And he really is rather shy, you're quite right. You see, he's not from here but from a small village that hardly exists anymore, twelve kilometers away, so that he's hardly seen any foreigners during his lifetime. So you must forgive him for staring at you so. It isn't hatred, it's astonishment.

Hatred? I ask, why should it be hatred?

I thought that was what you thought it was.

But why should I, I exclaim. And why is he so astonished?

Oh, that's simple, the supervisor says. It's because you've undertaken such a long journey just to see him. For naturally he thinks you've come because of him. *Vieni qua,* he exclaims, and before I can explain to him that the staring doesn't matter at all to me and I can do without the handshake, the supervisor takes the boy a few paces aside and is talking down at him rapidly from behind the wide, padded shoulders of his black jacket, with his thick fingers, which first he licks, patting the boy's uncombed black hair into a sort of coif around his head.

I want to go home, my wife says.

Yes, I say, but surely not now.

Yes, she says, I want to go home now.

But he's invited us, I say.

And what's he doing with the boy, she asks. What's he muttering to him?

He wanted him to shake hands with me, but instead the boy put his hands in his pockets. Like this, I say, and I imitate it for her. Now he's probably explaining to him that it wasn't polite.

And why pull his hair, she asks.

But he's not pulling his hair, I say, he's just making him look nice.

Why, she asks.

Well, so he'll look decent.

All the same, she says, after a moment's thought, I want to go home.

Home, the supervisor exclaims, for in spite of the distance he can hear everything and has immediately turned from the boy to face in our direction, but why home, it's going to begin at any moment. We've had our talk, he realizes how to behave with a foreigner now. Yes, he exclaims and hobbles back to us, if they hadn't got me, what would they do? And you can speak in front of him, he says, no problem, he doesn't understand German. He doesn't understand anything, not a word, and he can't read, either. I'm only saying this in case you want to talk about the impression he makes on you, or ask me questions. For instance, how he got the scar on his forehead. And when I wave him away, not wanting to talk about the impression the boy has made on me, he brings little Mimiddu, who has bowed his head, toward us again, this time not by the neck but with a free arm laid over his shoulders. Yes, they're like animals, he says, you have to take a firm hold on them. A firm hold, important. Like this, he says, and shakes the boy forcefully a few times by the shoulders, to show us how, in his opinion, such a boy has to be taken hold of.

Careful, my wife exclaims, he'll hurt him.

Yes, I say, do be careful now.

Hurt, how can anyone hurt such a creature, the supervisor exclaims, and he shakes the boy a bit more, to show how much he can stand.

Careful, my wife exclaims, it's only a child, he's really hurting him.

Nonsense, the supervisor exclaims, and he shakes the boy again.

Listen, I say, and put my hand on his arm, my wife doesn't like to see what you're doing. You know how women are. At once they think you're doing God knows what kind of harm or hurting someone.

She thinks I'm hurting him, the supervisor exclaims, looking at me in astonishment. Does she really? But *how, signora,* he exclaims, turning to face my wife directly, meaning to dispel her doubts, how would I hurt him? And where, he exclaims, hurt him where?

But my wife at this point turns away from him and turns her back on us. And then, so as not to see how the boy is being shaken, she even walks a few paces away from us, her head to one side, as if she didn't belong with us, standing on the edge of the area and looking up at the tower.

See what you've done, I say. You've offended her. Look how she's turned her back, she doesn't want to have any more to do with us. Yes, I should go to her now, actually, and look up at your tower, too, I say, but I don't go, no, I go on looking a bit more at the way he's shaking the boy.

Offended, how can I have offended her, the supervisor exclaims, and for a moment he stops the shaking. And *where* should I be hurting him, *where*, he exclaims, and he resumes the shaking again.

Well, I say, and I look at the boy once more, and since, of all the parts of his body his long and delicate throat seems to be most endangered, I say: Well, perhaps his throat.

His throat, the supervisor exclaims and he starts to laugh, certainly not his throat. Look, he exclaims, and lets go of the shoulder, to put his paw on the back of the boy's neck again and now shaking his throat. Only to show how hard one can shake, how firm such a throat is. Take my word for it, he exclaims, they're tough, especially their throats are. And then to the boy, letting him go: *E adesso dai la mano al signore.*

The way the boy extends his hand to me, gazing at the ground, so that one can't see his face, shows me that he must have spent a lot of time begging at church doors.

Ma, guarda negli occhi del signore, quando te lo dico, the supervisor exclaims, still standing behind him, even if he's not shaking him anymore. And then the boy raises his head, so that I'm able to see his face for the first time at close quarters. I'm thinking at once: Poor Mimiddu! Because, as I'd suspected, he's of the tribe of those unwanted, downtrodden, and superfluous creatures in this world who are born old and even when they're children they have the envious and calculating looks of adults, the pinched mouths, the creased foreheads, veins on the backs of their hands, yellow smokers' fingers, et cetera, et cetera.

How many times in the past, before you were married, in the most various countries, even where one would never have anticipated it, I'm thinking, you've studied such children's faces, their color always almost ashen, pallid. And placed your slightly awkward hand on their warm heads. The color of Mimiddu's face, too, is almost ashen, pallid, a color I'd almost forgotten, but now discover again. But I don't lay my hand on his head, I'm older now. Too late, I'm thinking, too late. And that he probably belongs among the people who are lost. Most resourceful in inventing incredible gestures, the eyes shifty and shy, the gaze—like this one now—lowered to the ground, these children have mouths that give off a smell of corruption. Even the cheeks carry the marks. True, they still piss standing upright and proudly, and they shake themselves without constraint, but their hands, when they're asked to show them, tremble and are clenched. And from their grins you can see that they're ill at ease with being in the world. That's why, in the countries I've visited, they show themselves in daylight as little as possible, they crouch behind draughty doors, live in murky cellars and in the lofts of barns, where there's nothing else but dead birds. And when, after months, after years, we happen upon them again and lay a hand on their cheeks, they immediately feel guilty and slip away from under our hands. And this is the kind of child I'm face to face with now, just such a child is looking at me, speechless.

Sorridi un po' al signore, the supervisor exclaims.

Must get away from here at once, I'm thinking.

Because, in previous times, when I was single, on my

travels, it often happened that a boy like this would simply attach himself to me and follow me for hours, silently, with bowed head. And whenever, to get rid of him, I'd take refuge in a café or a shop, he'd sit outside, waiting in the sun, on a curbstone. And go on following me, the moment I came back on the street, like a dog, with doglike looks, through entire cities, and far outside them, and I didn't know how on earth to get rid of the child, always a few paces behind me, stopping if ever I'd stop. So that children who had nothing to do with me, in those times of my life, often pursued me deep into the night. Yes, they'd follow me even into my dreams, so that, to get rid of them, I'd sometimes have to break off my vacation, simply travel away.

Bene, I say to the supervisor, after I've pressed the boy's small and sweaty hand and let it go again at once, pushing it away, whereas Mimiddu doesn't press my hand at all, his hand just lies limply in mine, *bene.* And that, if he still had things to discuss with the boy, we wouldn't detain him but would go into the café now, to wait for the spectacle to start, surely it wouldn't be much longer. Don't you think? I say to my wife.

I want to go home, she says.

Now? I exclaim. Now that we're at the tower? Just when everything's beginning? Later, later, I say.

No, now, my wife says.

Oh, let her be, she hasn't been listening, a nuisance, I say. And I'm thinking she's adopted her unfortunately typical attitude: always wanting the contrary to what she's got. The supervisor and I, we wink at one another, as men

we understand one another. Right, I tell him, we'll go to
the café, see you there. And then to her, holding her by
the elbow: Come on, Maria! And I manage, without the
boy's following me—his gaze has long since been fastened
on the ground—to escape from the supervisor, who is
walking off toward the tower, and to reach the terrace of
the café, on which far too many tables and chairs have
been set up. For heaven's sake, where in this hole would
all the visitors come from, I'm thinking, as we walk among
the tables and chairs, which were at one time white but
now the paint has peeled away. Everything empty, everything empty. We now have three possible courses of action.
Either we walk to the end of the terrace and escape,
jumping over the low hedge into the cemetery which
begins at that point. And without looking around we'll
simply give the supervisor the slip, running over the
graves. But I'm fearing that it won't be so easy to escape
from him, from the tower area he'll be able to see us
running through the cemetery and over the graves. Or
we'll go into the café, sit down at a table and roll up our
sleeves, or else we'll stand at the bar and drink something,
a cold espresso for her, perhaps, and perhaps a glass of wine
for me. But since one doesn't much like sitting in a café
when it's so hot, and, on an evening like this it is also not
so good to stand at a bar . . . Or, third, we could just
glance inside the café, rapidly show our sweaty faces, and
then sit at a table *outside.* To wait *outside,* facing the
tower, for the start of the spectacle, which I can't imagine,
nor do I want to. I'll be careful not to repeat my mistake,
not to contrive in my head, as I did with the tower, some-

thing that doesn't exist. And as I step into the café and show my face, I see in the predictably low-ceilinged and dingy room that there really are people inside, a whole lot of people. Strange, after so few people, suddenly so many. Whereas on our walk through D. we'd come across three, perhaps, or four, all of them local people, all in isolation, now in the café it's a question of ten, or twelve, or twenty. What brings them here? All foreigners, as I can see, once my eyes have got used to the twilight of the café, and as I can hear by their voices. So of course I'm very surprised. Maria, just imagine, there are people here, the café is packed, I exclaim over my shoulder. But my wife, who's standing behind me, true, but whose thoughts are elsewhere, is not surprised, or at least she doesn't show it. What are so many foreigners doing in a dump like D., at such a time as this, I immediately wonder. For obviously their being here is no coincidence. It's also obvious that they're a group of tourists, however loosely associated. Yes, I tell myself, quite evidently, even if you think it's fundamentally impossible, they're here for the spectacle, why else? Evidently they've had themselves flown from Catania and have come the rest of the way in buses. You haven't seen their buses, I'm thinking, but they'll probably be parked behind the café. And that the spectacle, which I thought till now was a rip-off for tourists, not to be attended if avoidable, just might be something that appeals to some people and has even inspired them to make the journey into this dried-up interior of the country. They'll know why they're here, even if I don't, I'm thinking. And now, of course, I'm curious and I take a good look at these

people who have come here of their own free will, as good
a look, that is, as one can take, when people are sitting in
the dark. And immediately, I don't know why, I feel an
aversion to them. No, I'm thinking, not a nice sight. Ugh,
I'm thinking, how repulsive! Although I can hardly
identify them in the dark room. But perhaps this is partly
due to my prejudice against tourist groups. Not if I lived
to be a thousand would I join a tourist group, never. To
me such groups are, honestly, the pits, because I always
connect them with the worst evils, with noise, vulgarity,
dirty jokes, lewdness, greed, et cetera. And now there's a
tourist group in D. And what's more, a group whose
motive for traveling lies in the dark, in the dark of this
cramped lowdown café. A tourist group that is held
together by a curiosity, a craving to see something, a
voyeurism altogether foreign to me. *Oh no,* a tourist group,
I exclaim over my shoulder to my wife, but she doesn't
answer. Because, as I now see, she hasn't followed me to
the door of the café and isn't even standing behind me,
but is still on the edge of the terrace looking up at the
tower. The men of the tourist group in the café, and, to
make matters worse, almost all of them are men, all wear
dark clothing, even black neckties. Many are coatless,
having thrown their coats over chairs or hung them on the
wall, because of the heat, but since all wear expensive silk
shirts they can afford to be without coats. One, a tall
skinny Englishman with a hooked nose—but he might
also be a tall American—is in the process of distributing
small coins among a few children, but he doesn't put them
into their hands, he tosses them into the air, so that the

children with loud shouts fall upon every coin and shove
and kick one another aside with all the strength they can
muster. And the tall Englishman or American is standing
in the middle of them and laughing, doubling up with
laughter. As I said, not a pretty sight, but repulsive. And
me? Do I intervene? No, I check myself. Yet I do walk
farther and farther into the room, smoky and sweaty as
it is, full to bursting with stale air. For on the bar, on a
black dish, under a sheet of cellophane, there's a cut melon
at which I want to take a close look. A lot of flies have
already crept under the paper and are sitting on the
melon, but its juicy red fruit makes my mouth water. For
a long time I stand before the melon and study it, gaze
at it in astonishment. And licking my lips, I'm planning
to have a slice cut off for myself and to bite into it straight
away. And I'll order a second slice, a somewhat thinner
one, for my wife, and if she refuses it, as she probably will,
I'll eat that second slice too. But I can't order the melon
because there isn't a waiter. Among the clients there are
Frenchmen, Americans, two Japanese who are photograph-
ing one another, a Swiss with his wife who speaks German
but is unintelligible to me, and another Asian. And I'd
been thinking the café would be empty! Because I'd seen
nothing from outside, and since the village was empty,
I'd had no conception of the café being full, actually
packed. And as I lean against a wall I remember—don't
know why—my father, who at the same age as me now, in
a café just as packed as this one, collapsed suddenly and
was dead. Without ever comprehending that he was dying,
without ever comprehending himself and the world. And

now, my back to the wall, hands knotted behind me, hoping a waiter will come, through half-closed eyelids—the small figure of my father, dead, stretched out beside the bar, his tongue sticking far out of his mouth when we find him, all of which I now have to thrust aside, cover up, push away.

11

⊡ ⊡

⊡

The waitress, who as it later turned out is the mother of the proprietor or tenant of the café, is a small and irascible old woman with a deep stoop induced by so many orders and servings of food and drink, and, in a long flowing black dress, she suddenly emerges from the kitchen, pushes me out of the café the moment she sees me, grumpily follows me outside, and, with her dishcloth, not saying a word, waves us—my wife is there again!—toward a table. We're the first clients there. Too early, to cap it all, we've arrived too early. All right, we sit down. And I order, after a few gasps of relief—we're sitting down, finally sitting down?—a *vino rosso con gas* for me and an *espresso freddo* for my wife. But make it a strong one, lady, I call out to the old woman, forgetting the melon I also want to order. And I decide, as I take my cameras off and put them on the table before me, to order the melon as soon as she brings the wine and the coffee. With our hands shielding our eyes against the last, particularly fierce rays of the sun, we look around. A good view in all directions, even from the terrace—a landscape with many bushes, dense ground cover, also hills and rising gradually in the distance partly wooded and partly bare mountains. Beside us, in the cemetery, theatrical, greenish black cypress trees, rigidly fixed. And before us, in the empty area, the tower in all its hideousness, all its misery. How ridiculous, such a tower in such surroundings! How criminal, to build it outside the cemetery and then to forget it. And me, how intoxicated I was with thoughts of the tower, walking through the village! How I kept on thinking and talking about it! No, you won't look at this tower anymore, I'm thinking, and I turn my back on it. So where can I look now? At the cemetery, yes, at the cemetery. And while looking at the cemetery, which is very quiet, situated on the gentle upward slope of a hill, crisscrossed by narrow paths, I'm still thinking of the tower. Until I finally tell myself: Stop it now. Until I tell myself I must think of something more important. And what's more important than the tower? Your decision to leave her, of course. Which you're pushing around, feebly enough, in your mind, and which must finally come out. And all at once, looking at my wife sharply from the side, I have the decision on my lips—but I still don't come out with it. The lie that for years on end has been between us, and has to be! For instance, this lie of having the decision so long on my lips but not coming out with it. But instead of concerning myself with it, I've been rapidly thinking of the spectacle soon to come. Which, as soon as the supervisor comes back, we shall also have to admire and praise, with our legs stretched out beneath the table. In the village itself there seems not to be much interest in the spectacle. Probably people in D. have other cares. Slowly, as I now see from my table by the cemetery, D. is awakening from its deathly sleep. And while my wife drums on the table with her fingers, I'm following with my eyes a couple of girls walking unsteadily, hand in hand, looking down at the ground, as they emerge from their sleep, hair fuzzed out from their heads, along the slowly darkening village street, or rather, along the street in which the shadows are thickening. Then a beggar comes, with a tired dog, an old couple, married, or brother and sister, yawning and carrying a can, and another person also, absorbed in a dream. They're all walking into D. or out of it, as if there were no spectacle in the offing. Whereas the supervisor, surrounded by children, of whom I think as the *bloody ones*, hasn't forgotten the spectacle by any means. He has limped back to the tower, and, hands on hips, his cane propped at an angle in front of him, he postures. In a voice that's suddenly very loud and decisive, thus quite new to us, he is calling out to the top of the tower instructions which aren't being followed or understood by whoever is up there. So that two boys, both skinny, both dark-skinned and with strong white straight front teeth, have to go into the cemetery for him and bring a ladder, which he immediately takes from their hands and props against the tower. And now he's climbing it, dragging his left leg behind him, while the *bloody* children gape at him, but we also ungrudgingly watch, as he carries on, from the topmost rung, his conversation with the person on the tower, who turns out to be little Diagonale.

119

Look who's up there, I exclaim, It's little Mimiddu. Yes, it's the goat-killer, and his movements back and forth on the platform are far more assured than ours were. But the supervisor, a dark blob, even his cap is askew, seems almost unreal on his ladder, or he seems at least improbable, talking upward so obsessively. Even the heat seems not to trouble him, at least we don't notice it having any effect on him, even though he's now starting to knock on the tower with his fists, as vigorously as he can.

Look, I say to my wife, the supervisor, how he's knocking. And I ask myself—needn't ask her, she doesn't reply—why is he knocking like that? Is he testing his tower, to find out how stable it still is, how much strain it can take? Or is he knocking because little Mimiddu is slowly driving him to distraction? Because the boy, even though he's so close to him, isn't listening to his words of advice? Vigorously rubbing my leg I'm asking myself at my table, which is placed as if for obtaining the best possible view, whether this conversation, with a ladder up there, is really necessary. Yet this question doesn't concern me so very seriously. I'm just glad that we can take a rest and stretch our legs beneath a table, however wobbly it may be, after our long march. Now, too, the wine arrives, and the espresso. On the table the old woman places a wooden tray with the cup and the glass, together with a bowl of small sweet cookies, which we hadn't asked for. Just a moment, I say, but before I can order my melon she has rushed away again. Meanwhile other clients, as we now see, have settled at tables on the terrace, though at a distance from us. People here seem not to be very sociable, they prefer to sit separately. And the supervisor? I look up and he's climbing down the ladder again, coming now in our direction, having set his cap straight. It'll be starting any moment, he calls to us from far off, and he waves and comes shuffling closer, but doesn't stop at our table, he limps on past us. Eat, drink, refresh yourselves, all expenses are on me, he calls over his shoulder, and then he disappears into the café. To emerge again immediately, followed by the old woman, who must have been waiting for him inside the door and is carrying behind him, in spite of her age and stoop, a basin of water. Do you know there was going to be a grandstand here, the supervisor calls, pointing all around the terrace, with bleachers, just imagine.

With bleachers, I ask, how do you mean?

Well, he exclaims, sort of staggered.

Aha, I say, a grandstand.

Yes, he says, anyway that's what was planned. To enable the guests to follow the spectacle closely, study all the details. Originally we conceived of the whole thing on a bigger scale, you see.

Bigger, aha, I exclaim and move my chair closer, so as to understand what he's saying better.

Yes, he says, but then, thank God, we thought it over again and decided to wait for the bookings to come in first. Between you and me, it was disappointing. There was much less interest than we'd thought, and many bookings we'd counted on weren't made. So then we dispensed with the grandstand. Now of course we're glad that we didn't build it and spared ourselves the task at least. See how few people have come, isn't it a disgrace, he exclaims, and shaking his head he points to the many empty tables.

So you'd been expecting more, I ask.

Of course, he exclaims, many more.

Well, I say, I wouldn't worry, if I were you. It hasn't begun yet. Who knows, perhaps a few more people will come. And in the café, too, you won't have seen yet, probably you didn't go far enough inside, but in the café, way back at the bar, there are some people. And wanting to cheer him up a bit, I exaggerate and say: Almost a hundred!

No, unfortunately it's not a hundred, but there are a few, says the supervisor, who seems to have looked around in the café after all and to know what the situation is. Yes, he says, there are a few.

You only need to call them, I say, and the terrace will be full.

Well, he says, taking his necktie off, I appreciate your being so thoughtful about something which really doesn't concern you, but unfortunately your thoughts are somewhat beside the point. For first I don't need to call them, they'll come of their own accord, and second, the terrace still won't be full, unfortunately, even when they're all here.

But it'll be half full.

Well, it might be half full.

And that's enough for you, I ask.

No, the supervisor loudly exclaims, it's really not enough for me, but what can I do? Either there's less interest in the spectacle than we'd supposed, or the people responsible for making preparations have let us down.

Ah, certainly it's the people who've let you down, I exclaim, because I'm supposing he'd rather hear this, although of course I can't prove they've let him down. I don't even know what spectacle we're actually talking about. And I'm about to ask: Listen, Herr Hans, what spectacle are we actually talking about? But I save the question for later and say once again: Certainly it's the people who've let you down.

Well then, he exclaims, tossing on to a chair beside him the necktie he's been alternately scrunching and smoothing in his hands, in that case we know whose fault it is.

Whose? I ask.

Not mine, the supervisor exclaims, fairly loudly, I've done my utmost. Then he signals to the old woman for her to lift the steaming basin on to an empty table next to ours, and takes off his coat, gasping and groaning. His beautiful white shirt, just as I'd been fearing all the time, really is soaked in sweat.

Look how he's sweating, isn't it amazing that a person can sweat so much, I say quietly to my wife. It's exactly as I described it to you, even in the identical places. And since he can overhear us and I want to avoid giving the impression that we're speaking ill of him behind his back, I say once more, but now much more loudly and turning to him: See how you've been sweating, Herr Hans!

Yes, he says and looks down at himself with a certain pride. How right you are.

And you really do think that it's unhealthy, I ask. Couldn't you have simply taken off your jacket when you climbed the ladder just now? And since I'd still like to know why —as a precaution or in desperation—he was knocking on the tower, I add: If one knocks so vigorously one can't help sweating, in this heat. At least you could have taken off your coat, I exclaim. Then you could have avoided it, I add and point to his coat, which has thickly padded shoulders, to give an appearance of the breadth usual for men hereabouts. Such a hot climate, I exclaim, and such a heavy coat.

But I've told you I haven't got a lighter one, the supervisor now exclaims, almost angrily, and he hangs his coat, saturated with sweat and steaming slightly, over the back of a nearby chair. And being now so close to our table, without asking us he takes a handful of the small sweet cookies and crams them into his mouth, while shuffling back to his basin.

Did you see, his coat is as wet as his shirt, I whisper to my wife. Look how heavy it is. And because he's leaning over to listen, I exclaim: I was only saying that your coat is wet through. With sweat, I mean. No mistake about that, is there?

No, he exclaims, it's true.

So one can say so, I ask, can't one?

Yes, he says, one can say so.

All right then, I say. And seeing his grimy hands, black hairs on the backs of them—after studying them for a while, shaking his head, he plunges them deep into the basin—I'm thinking that he shouldn't have eaten the sweet cookies with hands as dirty as that. And with his sleeves rolled up, bending low over the basin, he now admits as much. Yes, you're quite right, he exclaims, his mouth full, one shouldn't eat with hands like that. There now, he exclaims, and pulls his hands out of the brew, so as to take another look at them himself, you'd think I'd been rummaging in the dirt all day. But I haven't. An hour ago, at about six, they were still spotless. It's just that everything here is covered in dust and dirt, covered in filth. And then, having found a piece of soap in the old woman's apron, he starts to wash his hands.

I wanted to ask you something, I say: do the people here understand us? I mean, do people understand, or can I talk openly? And to make my meaning even plainer, I point rather brazenly at the old woman, who has positioned herself between us, although she should be able to see that we're having a conversation or at least wanting to shout our remarks and thoughts to each other across the space between us. Also there's nothing left for her to do for us at the moment.

Oh, her, the supervisor exclaims and makes a dismissive gesture, she's not important, you can forget her. And besides, set your mind at rest, he says, gesturing now with both arms soaped up to the elbows, she doesn't understand German.

Aha, I say, so she didn't understand my question?

No, he says, she didn't understand that, either.

And does she understand what we're saying now, I ask, because the old woman is watching our lips attentively.

No, not that, either, he says. And even if she did understand German, she wouldn't understand, because she's also deaf.

Deaf too! I exclaim, and, in face of so much misery, I suddenly start laughing. I practically slap my thighs, finding the old woman now so comical. So she's deaf! I exclaim, over and over, so she's deaf!

Yes, the supervisor says, without sharing my hilarity, she's deaf, too.

Well, I say, after laughing inside myself for a while, it doesn't surprise me. I thought there was something odd about her.

And what, if one may ask, made you think that? the supervisor asks, earnest as ever.

Well, I say, it's simple—she keeps on looking at our lips. Also she seems to distrust everyone, but especially me. And earlier, when I wanted to order from her two slices of melon, a large and a small one, she didn't wait for the order at all, but simply went away, as if she despised us. Yet we're clients of hers. Yes, I say to my wife, you don't know it yet, but inside on the bar there's a wonderful melon, which has already been cut into, and I wanted to order us a slice each, but unfortunately nothing will come of it. Who knows, perhaps it's the only melon in the place, perhaps it's not for sale, I say, and I can't help laughing again. And then again to the supervisor? You know, I've got the impression now that what she'd like best would be to push us away from our table, into the cemetery, perhaps. And at the idea of the stooped and wizened old woman with her long thin arms actually pushing first me and then my wife into the cemetery, I laugh again, I just can't help it. Why doesn't she wait on the other clients or sit in the kitchen, if she's deaf and can't speak German, I ask.

Well, because she's waiting for me to finish washing my hands, of course, the supervisor says. I've told her she may take the dirty water away with her.

You told her? I ask, and did she understand you?

Yes, me she understands, the supervisor says, I simply make signs to her.

And why does she have to take the water with her, I ask, will it be used again?

No, of course not, the supervisor says, she'll take it with her into the kitchen, yes, but she'll take it through the kitchen and out again at the back and pour it on the ground behind the house, where it will trickle away.

Behind the house, where the buses are? I ask.

Yes, he says, that's where the buses are. But let's not bother about the buses and about what she does with the water, he exclaims, and since he's now finished washing his hands and is standing at the basin, he starts to wash his face too. As if to drink the water, he stoops low over it and throws whole handfuls of water, one after another, into his face. Actually he should have clean fresh water for that, I'm thinking, but probably there's none to be had here, either, or only very little, and I watch the way he splashes water on his face. And the way he soaps it, until there's a great froth everywhere. And all this time he goes on talking. Help yourselves, he exclaims through the froth, go on, help yourselves! Go on eating and drinking. You must eat and drink, he exclaims. And then, amid gasps and snorts as he soaps the back of his neck: You should have asked, at this point, whether the spectacle—and he points now to the tower, to indicate from which direction it's to be expected—is a local production, if that's the word . . . Yes, of course, that's the word.

. . . or, as is usually the case, financed by the provincial administration, if not from Rome. Well, he exclaims, making a particularly energetic, if not obscene gesture, we decided in favor of the more honorable though laborious solution, and we're doing everything ourselves, as you see. No money, nothing, you understand, and as I suddenly hear, or think I do, a strange sound in the distance—like circus music—he's pointing once more at the tower.

But of course I understand, I say and out of politeness I too look up at the tower again, although I really don't always understand the supervisor and haven't been listening to him attentively for a long time. For I'm familiar now with everything he's capable of saying and thinking. Also in this heat, even sitting down and stretching one's legs, it would be difficult to follow foreign trains of thought, if they really were new. It's even difficult to collect one's own thoughts in such a climate, at least for me. And my poor wife now, too, in her condition! She's long ago given up listening to the supervisor's remarks and is completely wrapped up in her own concerns. She leaves it all to me, to talk with him and deal with him. In fact I sometimes wonder if she's good for anything now. On the other hands, the old woman, still there, even if we keep on talking past her or over her, listens carefully to what the supervisor says, especially when he's pointing to the tower, and does try to decipher what he says.

No, no money, everything out of our own pockets, the supervisor exclaims again, and he lets the dirty water run off his arms, while in the distance, coming out of the village of D., the strange grinding and tinkling and scraping we've been listening to gets louder. And just at the moment when I exclaim: Why don't you sit down and join us? there appears out of a side street, in a cloud of white dust, a small procession. Imagine, a procession in a place one thought was empty, dead, extinct! How easily one is fooled. Don't get excited, I say to my wife who, after one look, starts to breathe more rapidly and settles deeper into her chair. And I ask the supervisor, who has meanwhile found a towel, too, in the old woman's apron and has pulled it out, if this thing creeping toward us, no, sobbing toward us, might be the spectacle, and I could hardly suppress the horror in my voice.

The spectacle, the supervisor says, and he smiles faintly, no, it's not the spectacle yet.

Well, it could have been, I say.

No, he exclaims once more, drying first his face and then his hands, it's not the spectacle yet.

Well then, I was mistaken, forgive me, I exclaim, shielding my eyes with my hands, because of the sun, so as to get a better look at the curious procession. I sit up more erect, tighten my grip on the chair arms, but then, although I'm somewhat accustomed to things in these southern countries and always take a dismissive and skeptical, a *northern* attitude, I really am shocked when I see what's creeping toward us. It's a hunger march. Women and children, about two dozen, but old people too, all of them emaciated, decrepit, deformed, in loose, dark, ragged robes, the children rickety, probably sick with worms, if not tuberculosis. And this procession, which I won't describe in further detail, is creeping, as I clutch my cameras close to my body, across the tower area and is suddenly coming our way. In their hands they hold tin plates, cans, and saucepan lids, which they bang together. And in high, well-rehearsed tones, they are keening and whimpering.

If this isn't the spectacle, what is it? I say to the supervisor, trying to hide my horror, explain!

Well, the supervisor says, quickly drying his ears with a corner of the towel, in any case it isn't the spectacle.

But what is it? I ask.

Something else, he says.

But what? I ask.

I can't tell you that as quickly as you'd probably like me to—and with a slight bow he's standing at our table. Also before I tell you about it I'd like to put my coat on and tie my necktie, so I'll feel human again. And then, having tied his necktie and put on his coat, thereby restoring his previous broad-shoulderedness and robustness, he positions himself behind the vacant chair beside us, but still says nothing.

Why don't you sit down and take it easy, tell us all about

it, I say, and I push the chair across for him to sit on. And to my wife I say: Why don't we make a little room. And while the supervisor is turning away from us again and with a short leaden comb combing the hair from his forehead, I say to her quietly: Watch out for what comes next. Watch out for the claptrap he's going to troop out now. But you know you needn't make anything of it, nothing. And seeing her vacant face, which the day's events have made to look almost fishlike, I move a bit closer to her and say: Just keep calm, nothing will happen to you as long as I'm with you.

And then, after hanging the cameras around me for safety's sake and clamping the wrist-purse tight between my legs, I explained it all to her, the way I see it, that's to say, the way it is. I told her that beggary in this region is a public vice, which one does best to ignore, since after all nothing can be done to change the poverty. The moment you get involved and take it all seriously, I tell her, pointing to the approaching procession, you'll have had enough of the whole country, even of the whole world, because the whole world suddenly turns out to be a poorhouse, and inevitably that takes away your joy in everything. And I add that in instances like this one—I point to the procession—the misery is always exaggerated out of all proportion. So, for example, this thing creeping toward us, just like the *rod people*, whom because of your obstinacy you never did get to see, is just one of the usual bits of local theatricality—a scene, presenting hunger and misery. The people here, you realize, I say, while the supervisor is still busy with his hair, which he's trying with both hands to build up into the kind of hairdo he had before he washed, are by nature actors and they know—something we've long forgotten— how to exteriorize their feelings, but especially their sufferings, and by so doing to blow them up in ways that are impressive, to magnify them fantastically.

You mean, my wife asks, that everything is . . .

It's a performance, I just have time to whisper to her, for now the supervisor comes back, to sit down not beside us, no, but *between* us. In fact, although I've been sitting beside my wife all this time, he pushes his chair ruthlessly between us, separates us, drives us apart.

Just a moment, I exclaim.

Thanks, he says, I can manage.

What's going on, I exclaim.

Something the matter? he says.

Well, I say and move aside a bit, since he's now sitting there. Well, I say, I see you've freshened yourself up.

Yes, he says, fresh and clean again.

Well, in that case perhaps you can explain this to us, I say, and I point to the procession. What's it all about, I ask. If it isn't the spectacle you've promised us and have been talking about for hours, what on earth is it? Then, having quickly wiped his nose on his wet handkerchief, the supervisor exclaims: But you'll admit now that it's not artificial, won't you? And what is it? I ask once more, glancing over the sad procession.

People, he says.

Well, I say and can't help smiling a bit, people!

Yes, people, he says.

From here, you mean?

Yes, he says, from round about.

Well, I say and give a quick laugh—for a long time, as I can tell, my wife has been finding the whole thing painful, unbearable.

I mean, not dead, as you see, the supervisor says, but moving, and with his hand he makes a movement, as if turning a wheel. And he explains to us, while the sweat gathers on my forehead, because of the heat and because of the sight of the procession, while the procession unrelentingly creeps toward us, that this is a demonstration, of course, what else, a *manifestazione* of the most downtrodden, the poorest people of the region, whom I myself chose, he says, and assembled and instructed to come here today.

And why, I ask, did you assemble them?

Because, he says, somebody had to.

A demonstration, I say, and give a bit of a laugh.

Yes, he says, a demonstration.

And when I object that a demonstration in the village of D., in its dirty outskirts, is senseless, if not ridiculous, because it won't be noticed, there being no people, because, I exclaim, there isn't anyone to witness it, the supervisor sits up a little straighter in his chair and replies: *We* are the witnesses. Which I can't of course deny, since the procession keeps on coming closer and will soon reach us. But, I nevertheless exclaim, we're only *two* people.

That doesn't matter, the supervisor says.

You think two witnesses will be enough, I exclaim.

Yes, he says, two will *have* to be enough.

Bad witnesses, bad witnesses, I exclaim, wiping my forehead. Because, I explain to him, hadn't he realized it yet, we had troubles of our own spilling out all over, special troubles, so to speak private ones, very remote from this island and the troubles it has. For instance, I say, I've been cheated at a vital moment by my wife. How can you expect, I exclaim, that a public demonstration by people of another country would . . .

At which point he interrupts me. I've told you already that we expected more people, he says. But this is the first spectacle of its kind in D., so one has to be satisfied with the public one has got. And then, he says, the people will be coming out of the café and they'll study everything and take it all in and take photos, and then it'll be worth it.

Aha, I say, so it's all right to take photos?

Yes, he says, it's permitted.

And you assembled them, I say and wink at my wife.

Quite correct, he says, I assembled them.

Doesn't that mean, I exclaim, wrinkling my forehead, that the whole procession is an act?

Not at all, he exclaims.

I mean, we know there's a lot of misery here, I say. We've always known this, even if . . .

Yes, he asks.

Even if it was just hearsay.

You see, he says.

But this, I say pointing to the procession, it really looks

so picturesque, you know. And it is. For instance, there's a very old man who, in spite of the heat, has put a sheepskin over his shoulders.

So you like it? he asks.

Well, I say, and, just as my wife is doing, I drum my fingers on the table. And I almost reply in the negative, but since it's he who's assembled the procession and not wanting to offend him, I only say: Well, yes!

So you don't like it? he asks and pushes his hair back from his forehead, so as to pass a hand over his face more easily.

Well, I say, you know, we like it and we don't like it. And at the thought that the misery of these people could be as great as the procession represents it as being, I feel the sweat trickling down over my shoulders. And what are they demonstrating against, I ask, thinking to bring the matter rapidly to a close.

Against suffering, the supervisor says.

Against what suffering, I ask.

Human suffering, he says, big and small. So they're demonstrating against . . . many things, I say. And after a pause: If not, I exclaim, against . . . everything? And make with my arm a broad gesture, sort of including the whole globe.

Yes, that's about it, he says, and he gives me a few examples. Let's begin, he says, with ordinary things, so bear with me if it's banal. They're protesting against the high rents and high prices which "keep them under," against unemployment, which "forces them to live no better than animals," but also against heat and cold, drought and rain, as well as against an earth which produces no fruits and

135

a sea which produces no fish anymore. And then, of course, he says, against the main illnesses, as against death in general. Against death, I exclaim, and start to laugh. Did you hear that, Maria? And because I just don't get it, I go on laughing a bit longer, but uncertainly.

Your husband is right, *signora,* this is a demonstration *against death,* the supervisor says, turning now to my wife, and saying this he places his hand unabashedly on his sexual organ. Death, he adds, to which people here are very devoted, you see, Oh yes. They love and honor death more than copulation and birth. And had we, during our stay—you've been here a few weeks, he says—in any way made *his* acquaintance?

Have we . . . ?

Yes.

With . . .

Right, he says, with *him.*

No, thank God, I say. No no no, not at all. But of course not, I finally shout, what a question! Yet I'm not so certain, nor probably is my wife. For right after arriving on the island, right after visiting the cathedral at Noto, which we'd toured with a guide and about a dozen other tourists, just after we'd left that baroque building—early eighteenth century—through the left-hand side door, which led into a park, and while our guide was drawing our attention to the ruins of the baptistery hidden among the oaks and pines and cypress trees, we had seen, my wife and I, although it was twilight, yet it was clearly visible, hanging in one of the trees, it was a fir tree, a man, all in black, and we had pointed him out to the guide, first in English,

then in German, immediately flabbergasted, no, shrieking and horrified, with arms outstretched. But instead of looking into the matter and going to the fir tree, giving the man a shake and perhaps cutting him down, the guide, suddenly clapping his hands, had hurried us all back as fast as possible into the cathedral and through it and out again by the main door and shoved us with his hands into our bus and out into the evening city traffic. So I'm not certain about it, nor is my wife. Was there a man hanging in the fir tree in Noto, yes or no, yes or no? Or was he standing on a ladder, yes or no, yes or no? Yet why, toward nightfall, in a fir tree, should a man stand on a ladder? In any case this man, whom I've thought about a lot and to whom I've repeatedly referred in conversation with my wife, the way he hung, stiff, unless I'm mistaken, in the branches of a fir tree, has stuck fast in my memory, so that the question, whether we'd had any acquaintance with *him* . . . No, no, I exclaim, what a question.
About what?
If we'd had any acquaintance . . .
With *him*.
No, no, I exclaim, no, no.
Well, the supervisor says, placing two fingers on his waxed mustache and pausing briefly, we can do . . . And after hesitating a little: Do something about that.
Meaning?
I mean, he says and suddenly gives me a sharp and impudent look straight in the eye, perhaps you might attend a . . .
What are you talking about, I exclaim.

Anything can be arranged, he says.

Like what, I ask.

A funeral, he says.

What do you mean, I ask.

Then suddenly the supervisor shouts, spreading his arms, as if about to burst into song: Nothing more spellbinding than a funeral in D.! And all at once he's going into raptures about burials here, especially of children. The slow pace and the shuffling of feet, keeping step, behind the small white coffin which lies light as a feather on the shoulders and has to be firmly held so that it won't fly up to heaven of its own accord. The mourners, loaded with flowers, completely absorbed in their sorrow. The music of brass instruments shining all golden and preceding the little coffin along the parallel path. For from D. to the cemetery, he tells us and points toward it, parallel with the village street there's a small path, seldom used, except that we hadn't yet known of it, but that's not the main thing. The sun brooding over the earth, brooding of heads over the world. The emotion surrounding it all, over the fresh grave, and all around the priest who, gathering up his robe, suddenly sinks to his knees and sings! Yes, a funeral like that is a thing to spellbind people, he exclaims and his paw is still resting on his member. An experience, he says, not to be missed. But had we other plans?

Yes, I say.

Aha, he says. Nobody is free, the holiday season will soon be over and work calls, is that it? he asks.

Yes, I say.

Work can't wait, he says, although it could, just a few
days, since the experience is unique.

No, I say, the work can't wait.

So you'll be wanting to leave, he asks, scratching at his
mustache with a finger.

Yes, I say, we will.

Soon, he asks.

Tomorrow morning, I say.

And it can't be put off a single day, so that you can take
the other thing with you?

No, I say firmly and seriously.

All right, he says. In that case, so much for the unique
experience. It was only a suggestion, and there's no fatality
at present anyway, no dead child. Yet before you leave I'd
advise you in any case, he says, finally letting go of his member now, still to take some photographs of our poor people.
They've never been photographed before, at least not as a
crowd, and of course they're expecting it. So go ahead, it's
permitted, he exclaims and leans back a little in his basket
chair, making room for me to stand up. Then he pulls a
pack of cigarettes from his pocket, extracts a cigarette and
after tapping one end on the hairy back of a hand he lights
it. And I stand laboriously up, peel the leather cases away
from the cameras, give my wrist-purse to my wife, so as to
have it out of my way, and position myself beside the table,
with knees a little bent, to focus on the procession. Which
now reaches us and stops, so that we can also *smell* it, just
in front of us, forming a picturesque group; thus—the
children with pallid, pointy faces in front, behind them

the older and agèd people, staggered according to size and degree of misery, so that the tallest and the most miserable too, leaning against one another, appear at the upper edge of my viewfinder. Good, I'm thinking, excellent. Some of them hold up their pots and pans, chanting something, singing something. What's that? I ask, singing? A song?

And the supervisor, leaning back slightly and blowing the smoke from his mouth in small rings, says: Yes, it's singing. And what are they singing, I ask and bend my knees some more.

And he, legs apart, his cane planted between his feet on the ground: Songs, of course, songs. Did I like them?

But I don't understand them, I exclaim, aiming my camera purposefully at the group now.

Well, the supervisor says, they made them up. To exalt their misery in the words and to find comfort in singing, comfort which they did for the most part find, because of the many vowels in their language, but it was only temporary and there was never enough of it.

Quick, quick, Herr Hans, I exclaim, tell me what they're singing. And I start to shoot.

Well, for instance, the supervisor says, placing his hand once more on his member, they're singing: *None who did not escape From birth escape from death. He goes before who first Drew his last breath.* Or: *What's there for you to take, Death, from my empty room?* Or: *All the dead smell the same.* Or: *Fate, Fate, you give a ripe melon to some, to others an unripe melon.* Or: *Even the dogs are sad.*

Even the dogs, I exclaim.

Yes.

Then, as I continue to shoot, standing up, then crouching again, first one camera pressed to my cheek, then the second, vertical shots and horizontal ones, I again have the impression he's making fun of me, sitting there in his chair. I mean, why else should he . . . I mean: The dogs! The dogs! But he insists they're singing: *Even the dogs are sad.*

12

▢ ▢

▢

So it happens that we, my wife and I, after I've shot one whole roll of the folks, and taken, I hope, a few good pictures, and once the people in the café, attracted by the strange singsong, have groped their way blinking and unsteadily from the dark café into the pink evening light and called, they too in turn, for their cameras, to photograph *Misery with a Song*, while we, my wife and I, but the supervisor too, dispose ourselves at the foot of the tower in our basket chair—they look as if they've been pecked by vultures—and sink deep into our thoughts, each into his own. . . . What my wife is thinking I've no idea, and I'm not interested anymore, either, whereas the supervisor, sitting there with his legs apart, has anxieties much as I do. For suddenly he's serious and taciturn and he wrinkles his forehead, on which, in spite of his big wash, fat drops of sweat are again standing. And me, sitting down again: What am I thinking? What am I thinking? For a long time, with arms and legs spread out far from me, I don't know why I've been thinking: Thank God the tower platform is empty now and the boy down on the ground again. So I was looking around for Mimiddu among the tables on the terrace, which are filling now, and I don't see him there. He's still at the top of the tower and walking about on the platform, but in a lost sort of way—he's pulling at his shorts, his thighs are shining gold—careful now, young fellow! His dark hair falls over his forehead and he keeps tossing it back with a gesture of the head that we've come to know. Suddenly he's looking—or am I wrong?—in my direction, down at our table. Can he have recognized me? Does he want to flirt with me? On the table before me the wine I shouldn't have ordered, because it wreaks havoc in my head, but at which I'm still sipping, I sign to him with an index finger. Hey you, the finger says, and I look up at him, but he doesn't understand me. And then, as I might have expected, he has turned away again—a weariness overwhelms me. Too hot, much too hot, I'm thinking. I shut my eyes, no, they shut of their own accord, my chin sinks to my chest, a thread of spittle, as I'm later told, runs out of my mouth. In fact, I fall fast asleep. Flight through the cemetery being impossible, I try to escape from the supervisor into sleep. But soon he catches up with me.

Wake up, *dottore*, he exclaims and nudges me.

Yes, what's up? I exclaim and give a jump, opening my eyes.

Che cosa fa, vergognoso, he whispers to me softly, as if I'd done something forbidden, even obscene, something not to be revealed in these surroundings.

Yes, I say, what was I doing?

You were sleeping, he whispers.

No, I wasn't, I say.

Yes, you were, I saw it myself, he says, giving me a sharp look. First your chin sank to your chest, then your breathing slowed down, then came the sounds.

What sounds, I ask.

Well, the sleeping sounds, he says and waves around in the air a bit, as he says so. And wipe that away, quick, wipe it completely away, he says, pointing to my mouth. You didn't even notice. If I hadn't nudged you, you'd be in the middle of a dream now.

Nonsense, I say, and I wipe the spittle from my mouth, I was only thinking.

Thinking? he asks, doubtfully, what about?

I don't know anymore.

You see, he says, it's because you were asleep.

Nonsense, I say and sit up straight, to pull myself together again. You may have thought I was asleep, but in fact I only had my eyes closed, because there was something important I wanted to think about.

And what was the important thought, he asks, giving me a sharp look.

I don't know anymore, I say. I wasn't even able to think about it. You nudged me. Well, the supervisor says, if you've forgotten about it so soon, it can't have been so important. In any case, you can't fall asleep now, any moment the spectacle will be beginning.

Ah yes, the spectacle, I say, and I yawn again loudly, making an even worse impression, if possible, on the supervisor. *Mi dispiace, scusi*, I say and put my hand over my mouth. And then, to appease him: But I haven't forgotten about the spectacle, I say. If it's starting, I certainly won't sleep, I'll be paying attention all right. And to show him how alert I am, I sit up even straighter and look around in all directions. I even look up to the sky, which is the same unchanging blue, I even look behind me. And now I realize that I must actually have slept a bit, because things around us have changed utterly since I sat down again.

Just look, Maria, I say.

And now I admit: The supervisor has organized everything better than I'd thought. Quickly and invisibly in that short time he had assembled a public more than ample enough for such a spectacle.

Just look at all the people, I say to my wife.

And in fact the public now assembled is much bigger than I'd allowed myself to dream in my boldest estimates. The tables, the chairs, even the ground, all are filled and occupied. Evidently there'd been more people in the café than I'd thought. But of course it does make a difference, whether people are standing pent up in a low-ceilinged room, through to the far side of which we'd hardly been able to see, or walk outside and spread over a large area that can easily be surveyed in a good light. Outside in the open, I say to my wife, one realizes: There are more here than one had thought inside, in the darkness.

You've been dribbling, my wife says and points to my chin. Still? I say, and: Sorry! And I wipe it all away. And now

I admit that the supervisor had been right about the grandstand—there really should have been one. But without needing to be prompted, the visitors have spread out over the terrace *as if they were occupying a grandstand.* They've lined up in rows the white seats and armchairs from around the tables, and because the ground isn't quite flat but slopes slightly up from the tower area to the café, one has the impression of a natural grandstand, such as the supervisor probably envisaged in the first place. And as soon as it was realized that there wouldn't be enough chairs, others have been brought out of the café, or from behind it, little wobbly metal frames with spindly legs, so as to fill the ranks and extend the rows. And on these chairs they're now sitting, the gentlemen from the over-developed countries, who, for reasons unknown to me, have had themselves flown in here. Even though it's still very warm, they're all wearing black coats and black neckties. Their backs concave, eyes wide open, legs stretched out in front of them, they're sitting behind us, with wan faces, like ours, maybe even feverish. And their arms which are long like mine dangle to the ground, into the dusty grass. Many have brought from the bar their glasses of wine or liquor, their cups of coffee, to pass the time more easily until the start of the spectacle, of which there's still no sign. So as to have them always close at hand, they've set their drinks on the ground beside them, and now and then they sip them. Local interest, too, seems finally to have been aroused, for villagers have joined us and are greedily swallowing their own colorless home-baked cookies, which are sweet but extremely dry and plain. Eventually, since I can't stand the silence between us anymore, I remark on this fact.

Look, I say to my wife, the other foreigners aren't eating the cookies, either.

I want to leave, my wife says.

But there's no question of leaving now, even if we wanted to, the crowd is too big. More and more spectators are coming out of the village, singly or in groups. As soon as they arrive they stand on tiptoe and beckon to others, newly arriving, far away, calling out to them to hurry, because it's beginning. What's beginning? Nobody tells us, but we also don't ask anybody. There's really not much talk at all. Certainly there are several people here who know one another and who know what's going on, but others have no idea whatever and are wondering if they were right to come. Also the *bloody children* have suddenly shown up again.

Confused, their hands deep in their pockets, heads lowered, mostly in couples for safety, they walk through the rows of chairs and climb, without apologizing, over cups, glasses, feet. Some of the spectators know them, call to them, beckon them closer, whisper a few words to them, put coins in their hands or cookies into their wide open, always voracious mouths. Others put hands on their heads or tickle their ears with grass blades. Bewildered and awkward the children shut their eyes and let it all happen. Mimiddu is suddenly there again, too. Hadn't I just waved to him? Hadn't he been up on the tower? Has he perhaps seen the sign I made to him, after all? Anyway he's back among us, the most popular child of all. Heads gone gray or bald feel lighter at the sight of him, people turn toward him, point toward him, and word goes around that Mimiddu, in khaki shorts and a white shirt, has appeared in our midst. With straw sandals on his feet, and on the left one, I think, a green fragment of glass hangs by a thin silver chain. Very serious, very nervous—at your age, boy! —he gives a strained smile, bobs through the grandstand, answers all questions with a shake of his head, but lets himself be grasped, touched, on the hands, arms, shoulders, head, although he's embarrassed by this. Sometimes he almost starts to talk, begins a longish, rather confused speech, which he put together long ago, but then he retreats into himself, doesn't smile anymore, and so moves on, inwardly far away, past everything, with a serious look on his face. Then, in the course of his walk, he sees me at my table and comes toward me, holding out his hand. *Una sigaretta, per favore*, he says, without looking at me.

A cigarette? I shake my head. I don't smoke, I say, lying. The fact is: I don't want him to smoke, make a habit of it. And I explain to him why. It would be bad for you, Mimiddu, I say and jokingly threaten him with a finger, while my wife, who finds the conversation painful, looks away and up to her tower. Then, using my hands, which I stretch out and close and place one upon the other, I try to portray, to perform for the boy the harm that comes from smoking. I'm indicating his lungs, his heart, his nerves.

Non capisco, he says.

148

Perchè non capisci, I ask and explain to him that if he smokes a lot he won't grow but stay just as he is, get even smaller, perhaps. Wouldn't it be more sensible, instead of smoking, to take a bite to eat, a few of these little cookies? And turning to my poor wife, her cold shoulder, I say: What are you turning your back for? Why don't you offer the child some of your cookies?

And why don't *you* offer him, she says, some of *your* cookies?

Why should *I* offer them to him, I exclaim.

But then the supervisor is jabbing at the air with his hands, and he exclaims, breaking into our talk: No, don't offer him anything, no. *Non mangia più.*

What? I exclaim.

No, he exclaims, *non mangia più.*

So then we don't offer him anything. And although he's standing close beside me and my wife is still looking up at her tower, I don't stroke his hair or his arms, either. Yes, a curious shyness prevents me from even looking into his face. The supervisor behaves quite differently, shows none of my diffidence. He simply takes the boy by the elbow, simply pulls him and places him simply between his thighs, holds him simply tight between his thighs. Do you realize, he says, that he doesn't even know the alphabet? Not even the beginning of it.

Can that be so? I exclaim.

But he's sound, he exclaims, sound as a bell, except he's a bit thin.

Yes, I say, he really is thin.

Then the supervisor says: But take a look at his teeth,

don't just look at his ribs! And before the boy can stop him, he sticks a finger into his mouth and pulls his lips apart, so that I may see his teeth.

Yes, yes, I say, he's got nice teeth, I'd noticed them already. Yes, I say, he looks sound.

Doesn't he now, the supervisor says, taking his finger out of little Diagonale's mouth and wiping it on his trousers. Do you remember what I told you about him?

That he can't speak German? I ask.

Nonsense, he says, I said they're like animals, wild animals, only much less useful.

You think so, I ask.

Of course, he says, of course. But I don't tell him so, I let him feel it. And he puts his paw on the boy's shoulder, to scratch around on him a bit more. And while he's doing this he says in a monotonous incantatory voice: Mimiddu, a good boy, a brave boy. *Un ragazzo,* he suddenly exclaims, *che non ha paura, vero?* But Mimiddu, whose eyes have closed, perhaps because of the monotonous blue sky, still flushed with sunlight, perhaps too because of the monotony of the voice speaking so close to him, doesn't reply, only his lips are trembling. *Ho detto che non ha paura,* the supervisor says once more and gives his cheek a little pinch. Then the boy starts to tremble a bit more violently, not only his lips but his entire narrow head, his shoulders too are moving. Then his eyelids open again, only a crack, showing the whites of his eyes, and from between his lips, his teeth, a few sounds issue, words perhaps. Which I can hear, and perhaps guess at, but I can't understand them. *Ho detto,* the supervisor says, *che non ha paura.*

150

Sono morto, the boy perhaps says.

I'll describe him as he stood at our table, between the supervisor's thighs. Height: perhaps one meter fifty. Weight: perhaps ninety pounds. The face longish oval, hair black and curly and falling over his forehead into his eyes, which are brown, speckled with gold. Complexion, once like honey, is pale, but the teeth, as far as can be seen when he's not speaking, are intact and straight in his moist boyish mouth, while the brow is smooth and slightly curved and entirely inscrutable. Either, I'm thinking, a herb and snail collector, frog hunter, olive picker, or snatcher of car mirrors, then pimp, then killer with a knife. These, I'm thinking, dear Mimiddu, are your prospects for the next five or six years.

Distinguishing marks: None, except for the scar.

Instead, a few more details about him, which I noticed *before the spectacle* and which stayed in my mind long *after* it. I mean the shining thighs and calves the boy had, which looked as if they'd been rubbed with lard. His handful of languid dark vowels, especially the very open *e*-sounds. His remoteness, his inaccessibility when—the supervisor has his eyes closed, my wife is looking up at her tower—I'm looking at him from my chair, for a few seconds, uninhibitedly, no, voraciously.

Then, released from the supervisor's thighs, he walks on through the grandstand, to be stroked and touched, and we remain at our table. A quiet time now, for clearing throats and feeling awkward. My wife and I, after this encounter . . . A good thing that Herr Hans is sitting between us. But it's impossible for us, my wife and me, because of the spectators behind us looking over our shoulders and hearing every word and, through the very walls of our skulls, shamelessly feeling what we feel, thinking what we think—and immediately they perceive *and judge,* judge *and reject* our fears, gestures, thoughts, our very breathing. . . . In brief, we can't be concerned anymore with our own problems, so we can't talk about our separation or even think about it on this hot, now less hot than oppressive, steamy late September afternoon in this putrid village of D., which has quite imperceptibly become a steamy, oppressive, breathless and speechless early September *evening* in D. The open blaze of the noontime has given way to a suffocating closeness. The evening heat, perhaps even worse than the heat of noon. And I'd be lost if I didn't . . . And that's how I always do it: In such circumstances I always tell myself *the story of the present moment,* whether I'm lying sleepless in bed or waiting in despair for a phone call or, as now, seated grudgingly in a basket chair with my wife and the other person. Always when I'm lost or almost lost I tell myself the story of my lostness, and it helps. First I ask myself if I want to listen to it, yawn, and tell myself: No! But then I persuade myself that I *must* listen, because there's no other way out. All right, quiet now. Shall I? And so I start. For instance, if I can't sleep I tell myself *that* I can't sleep, perhaps because there's a faucet dripping somewhere. And I tell myself, in my story, how it's dripping, that's to say, always on the same spot, whether it's somewhere in the house or inside my head. And now, in D., in the twilight, in my seat in the grandstand, I'm at such a loss that the first thing I pack into my story is, of course, the tower. For I know that the tower belongs in it, first and foremost. And I tell myself of the tower and how I'm sitting facing it and what a disappointment it is and how lost I am here and how at all costs I must get away from here. And then Mimiddu comes, who, I'm thinking, is a poor good-looking boy in your story and, with bowed head, straw sandals on his feet, a little chain on his ankle, he walks into your story across the tower area, over the warm paving stones. And vanishes through the iron door, which closes behind him. Then he skips, still in my story, through the stink of the stairwell, avoiding the hard and the soft, lightfootedly up the spiral stair. But that doesn't appear in my story, it's only suggested. When he walks through the hatchway into the open air and looks down on us, everyone in the grandstand in my story holds his breath. All eyes are aimed at the boy, especially at his legs. Why? Do people want to see him dancing? Yes, indeed, I stuff the most trivial things into my story *At the Foot of the Tower*, for those trivial things alone make it into a story, they alone . . .

13

Suddenly, without raising my eyes, without looking up, I know that something, I don't know what, perhaps a movement, so I'm telling myself, is taking place, has taken place, up on top of the tower. Something that was first in one particular place is now, I feel, in another place. What is it, I'm thinking. And suddenly, without looking or looking up, I know that Mimiddu Diagonale, having stood until now behind the guard wall, is standing *on* it. At once I remember what it's like to be standing at the top of the tower, even if it's behind the guard wall and not on it. The swallows, I'm thinking. At once I remember how I myself, with swallows whizzing around me, closed my hands on the rail, how in a slight breeze I stood on the tower, the earth far below me. Even the tops of the cypress trees underneath me I remember, and looking down on them. And how I told myself, because I felt dizzy: Just don't look down, just don't look down! And now I'm sitting below at my table and thinking: Just don't look up, just don't look up! All right, so I look up and everything is as I thought it would be. Mimiddu is standing on the guard wall with his legs apart and he's going to dance. Look, I say to my wife, the boy is standing on the guard wall, he's going to dance, I say. Watch out, I exclaim, don't look up. But it's too late, she looks up. Everyone, I notice, is looking up. The supervisor, his face reddened with his washing, his heavy eyelids drooping, his finger in his mustache, the Englishman, the old man, everyone. Yes, even the misery people, their procession having dispersed, now leaning against the wall of the café, are looking up wide-eyed to the tower, to Mimiddu. And suddenly —I turn around again, to study the people behind me, in solemn expectation they're all wearing dark clothes, many have put dark glasses on, so their eyes won't be seen, and their creased faces, moist with sweat, are erased, retracted by the twilight, the approaching darkness, since the sun sets here quickly and it will be dark any moment. So behind us there's a lot of pallor and stiffness, also many quivering mouths, eyes, deep in their sockets and staring, hands are being wrung, teeth are grinding, a chin juts out at an angle, et cetera, et cetera. And then at the sight of these stygian figures, with a foreboding of the onset of night, I realize to my unspeakable horror that in D., in the close atmosphere of this evening, everyone is hoping for an impressive, perhaps shattering, maybe artistic performance of a death, the doing of a *death act*. Yes, everyone hopes, let's face it, that the boy won't dance, but that he'll jump.

I want to leave now, my wife says. It's always the same: whether she's sitting or standing or running around, she says I want to leave now.

No, I say, not yet.

Then the boy, little Diagonale, who is exactly as I was telling myself in my story, thus wearing straw sandals and a white shirt open, as is the custom in this country, to the navel, so that the marvel of his ribs is almost entirely revealed, is standing up on the guard wall in a very strange posture, like this: Motionless, bolt upright, in the south wind coming from far away, frayed shorts encasing his thighs, his hands along the side seam, tensed and determined, certainly visible for miles, unmoved but not inflexible, thus as if carved in wood or stone, or poured in dark wax, that's to say, unnatural, with a touch of gold on his shoulders, while around his ankle hangs a little chain with a green fragment of glass dangling from it. And with a face that is defiant, mottled with vague shadows—which reflect movements in his mind. And the eyes are leveled on a point in the landscape that's remote from us, a point from which, even if it were the crests of a distant mountain range, his gaze is trying to force an answer.

What is he looking at, I ask my wife.

Yes, she says, I want to leave.

But she doesn't leave. Then I feel like turning around and looking, myself, for the point at which Mimiddu is gazing, but I don't. Later, perhaps, I'm thinking. And I have, although his gaze passes so high over us away into the mountains, into the sky, suddenly the feeling that this boy, whose name I suddenly find I've forgotten, is looking into my eyes—so that for a moment I shut them.

All right, I shut my eyes, close my eyes.

When I open them again, that's to say, I happen to find myself looking at the tall Englishman or American, who has for a long time been traveling with his green suitcase in search of unusual customs and practices, pipe in mouth, binoculars in his lap. With a single thought in his head: What monstrous thing can the world still offer you? Yes, of course, I'm thinking, that's why he's here. But why *our* car happened to stop just outside D., I do not and cannot know.

At this moment Mimiddu Diagonale, yes, that was his name, raises both his arms, like a conductor giving his orchestra the sign for a tremendous surge. *The child with the skull in his head,* as I tell myself. *The victim,* as my wife probably thinks. *One of the best horses in my stable,* the supervisor perhaps thinks, dabbing the sweat from his forehead. And the Englishman or American, his binoculars raised to his eyes, is telling himself: *At last, an example of this species.* Whereas for the Japanese he is "that"—the thing they want to have in their picture. So Mimiddu stands, up on the tower, probably in his own view the *hero,* and doesn't know what he should do. Should he climb down again from the guard wall or should he jump? And in fact at this moment, in this part of the world, face to face with this question, such a silence reigns that one can hear each of the various sounds—of the street, of nature, people, animals—quite distinctly. This is the mo-

157

ment I've been waiting for, on which everything depends. Your moment, I'm thinking. The moment to intervene, for nothing has happened yet. The moment to jump up and with a calm voice, the voice of reason, finally put a stop to this macabre joke that has gone on far too long. But then I'm too tired to jump up, and I'm too hot. Instead, I lie outstretched in my armchair, my heart thumping, wipe my forehead with an arm and stare speechlessly up at the tower. I don't intervene at all, I even yawn, yawn up at the boy. Whose loneliness, although all eyes are on him, is very great and still growing. For, he's telling himself perhaps, if I die now the world dies with me. So should I jump or not? But nobody tells him what to do. The whole audience in the natural grandstand, not moving a finger, gazes speechlessly and inexorably upward. And of course a lot of sweating goes with it. Don't jump, I'm thinking, don't jump! And I hold still and simply look and hardly dare to breathe. And even nature holds its breath, because Death casts his shadow before, over the forests, over the sea, but also inside houses, where Death casts his shadow over carpets and furniture. And of course outside this café, because of the old dog, who, in the manner repeatedly portrayed by the great painters of Death, can smell death, can bark at him, and with hackles raised must finally back away, yielding to Death's stronger will. So now, where's the dog? With quivering flanks, tongue hanging out, he's lying in the dirt at our feet. Since he's completely emaciated, one can see the beating of his heart. But he's not smelling any death, and he doesn't back away.

No, it can't be said that nature is holding its breath to-night, nature goes on breathing as usual. Nothing's going to happen, I'm thinking. Of course, *the boy is an artist.* And that's what I say.

Don't be afraid, I say, and point to the dog, nothing's going to happen. The boy's an acrobat, it's all an act, rehearsed. Every step he takes, every step.

And then, the moment I say this, I've hardly finished the sentence, something horrible happens. The moment I say it my wife, who since the day first began, when in my anger at her pregnancy I told her of my illegitimate child, has been inundated with horror, drowning in it, but has sat there quietly and withdrawn until now, without mak-ing a movement or saying a word, not even uttering a sound to anticipate what now happens—amid all the hu-man sounds around us not a one has come from her—briefly, she swoops suddenly leaning much too far over the pecked and plucked right arm of her basket chair, like a hawk, the image shoots through my mind, swoops upon the fleshy red hand of the supervisor, which until now has been hanging limply over the left arm of *his* pecked and plucked chair, she jerks the hand with a speed beyond my comprehension—my wife, my wife!—to her mouth and bites into it. The supervisor, more exhausted by his preparations for the spectacle than I'd thought, as it now turns out, and who has allowed her to take his hand, artlessly, though now surprised, with eyebrows raised, utters a few deep sighs and then starts to tremble. But for a long time he doesn't realize what's happening, he's still thinking about it. This pain, where is it coming from, he wonders, perhaps, this pain you feel, what's happening with my hand?

Signora, he finally says, taking a deep breath and looking confusedly at my wife, but you're biting me. *Signora,* he says, stop! And then to me: *Signore,* look, your wife, see what she's doing to me.

Slowly clawing at the arms of my chair, the cameras in my lap, I raise myself up out of my stupor, annoyed that I should have to look away from the tower, raise myself up out of the grave of my chair, and I too am astounded. How strange, I'm thinking, your wife, what's she doing there? And think at first that she wants, God knows why, to kiss the supervisor's paw, but then I see there's blood running from her mouth. Blood, how strange! A fit, or a *raptus,* I tell myself, which had to come, after such a long silence, such prolonged restraint. And that I'd actually been expecting something horrible of this kind and magnitude from her, if not of course exactly this horror that's now happening. And I tell myself, you must do something, but what, but what? Maria, I say, reaching out my own hand, which is very limp with the heat, and laying it on her arm, what are you doing? You're hurting the gentleman. She certainly is, the supervisor with his unnatural width and scarlet in the face agrees at once, that's right, she's hurting me. *Signora,* stop it, he gasps, but quietly, because he doesn't want to attract attention to us—the other spectators are so absorbed in gazing at the tower that they don't even notice the biting. Look, *signore,* the supervisor says, turning to me once more, she's really hurting me. You think it's only a joke perhaps and she's only teasing me and biting gently, but that's not so, she's biting as hard as she can.

Maria, I now exclaim more loudly, but not nearly as loudly as I should have done, listen, what are you doing? You're hurting the gentleman! Stop it, I say. Come on, let's leave! And as she doesn't make a move: Come on, we'll leave now.

And as my wife still doesn't listen and now wants not to leave, either, but to go on sitting on the terrace and biting him, the supervisor again, bouncing up and down in his chair with the pain—the pleasure, I'm almost thinking— She won't stop! She won't stop, she won't even think of it! Do something, he exclaims, she'll soon get to the . . . Ahhhhh, he shouts, the bone! And he suddenly topples, no longer red in the face but white as his shirt, laying his right hand over his left, as if it were time to say a prayer, out of his chair on to one knee, under the eyes of the grandstand—which, however, are looking up at the tower, and now he's imploring my wife from the ground below. Ow, he exclaims and threshes about on the grass, looking at his hand in horror, and then at me and then at my wife, then at his hand again. Ow, he exclaims, it hurts! Ow, he exclaims, if you just knew! And this man, with his artificial width, still kneeling in the grass, he straightens up with pain, higher and higher, till he's reaching up as high as he can, and then he collapses again. Really, he exclaims, and from right down there he turns toward me, you have no idea how she bites. It hurts terribly. Perhaps you think I'm exaggerating because I'm a Sicilian, but I'm not. And he looks, closing his eyes and opening his mouth so wide that I can see his tonsils, as if he really were inordinately exaggerating his pain. O *signora,* you shouldn't do such things, he exclaims, and he shakes his head. And then letting a few tears trickle down his cheeks, to me again: Oh yes, your wife bites very painfully. And then, with as little warning as when she seized it—not much time has passed, but what a time!—my wife lets go of his hand. And pushes it away from her, and, blood on her mouth, subsides into her chair, says not a word, doesn't move, while the supervisor confusedly stays kneeling before her a little longer and then, in a dignified manner, though peevishly, slumps back into his chair. And only when the spectacle will have ended, when we're on our way to the hotel, pursued by the supervisor through the *vicoli,* will she wipe the last traces of his blood from her mouth.

For the child will be jumping any moment now. His arms outspread as if to fly, his gaze fastened on the sky, his face darkened by shadow, having looked at the world—us, us! —for the last time, Mimiddu takes half a step back on the guard wall, but lowers his arms again. A sigh of annoyance, of disappointment sweeps through the grandstand. So after all he won't jump? Good, I'm thinking, so he won't jump. And I'm disappointed, like the others. What's up, I'm thinking, is he going to jump at last, or not? Why does it all take so long? What are we waiting for? Get it over, jump, I'm thinking. And in fact, as if he'd heard my thought, after a last concluding sort of look toward the supervisor, who is wrapping his bloody paw in his handkerchief and then putting both hands—both hands!

—on his member, while for a long time the Englishman has had his binoculars trained on the boy, and the two Japanese, having already photographed everything and traveled from far away to see death at long last this evening, even if it's only a small death. . . . Well, the boy up there, while I'm preoccupied with the sweat that's pouring off me, bends his knees, leans forward a little, so as to have the right thrust for the jump, but then loses his nerve. And perhaps he really didn't want to jump, but now it's too late. Because of the thrust, which he tries to restrain, he has lost his foothold on the guard wall, lost everything, and now, without really wanting to be, he's in the air. Which, one thinks, should bear him up, but the warm air, although he spreads his arms and makes himself light as a bird and would like to soar like a bird, no, the air doesn't bear him up. So that now, even if he had wished to, he can't go back, but plunges, a dark wisp in a light shirt, and not even thrusting, as had been his intention, but meekly, a forlorn hopping creature, knees drawn up, a yell of horror in his mouth, the landscape gyrates wildly around him, his hair flutters, his fingers have spread, and he plummets to the earth, into death. With a brazen and incontestably final concluding thud, which stops the yell and which, I tell myself at once, you'll never forget, Mimiddu hits the tower area fairly flat, that is, simultaneously with many parts of his half-naked body. And because much of him is done for, as anyone can see, he remains there with strangely twisted outspread limbs, flat on his face. Finished, I'm thinking, finished, while everyone leaps up and amid screams and shouts and jostlings with elbows hurries either to the buses standing ready behind the café—the motors are running—or to the tower area, toward the boy. Finished, I'm thinking, finished. And still I can see—I too have jumped up, I want to get away fast—two elderly gentlemen turning him on his back with silver-chased canes, they stoop slightly over him, looking for the death-dealing wound. But this wound, soon to be covered with a black cloth of flies, I can hardly see it, it's concealed by the other people. Not paying for what we've had, I leave our table, choking back behind my clenched teeth disgust, sorrow, shame, and nausea, the airy cry still in my ears, also the thud, the splatting, and I don't bother about the supervisor, I follow my wife. Who, after she has jumped to her feet and doubled up three times in horror, like an animal unknown to me utters a loud howl, hand to her mouth, because she too feels sick, the other shielding her eyes, so as to see no more, and she's running very quickly, I can hardly keep pace, through the crowd that makes way for her, a hair's breadth ahead of me.

14

□ □

□

So then the same way as we'd come, crumbs from the pale-
colored cookies still on our fingers, above us now a night
sky with stars freely soaring in it, but with their better
order belonging in the space around the earth, and as the
supervisor, whom we ignore, hurtles after us shouting
Signori! through the natural grandstand, his cane in the
air, we ran with the taste of death in our mouths quickly
back to our hotel. We ran back through the same scenes,
thus at an angle across the *mercato*—here the supervisor
loses us—and past the small hole in the Foundlings' Home.
Shivering, with shirts buttoned up, we pass the *dammuso*
with the women in it, but where the window the supervisor pushed my head through is now shut and all is quiet
and dark. Only a whining, a little breeze, passes through
the *dammusi,* all of them. Whereas in the houses close to
the tower, old women dressed in black had been in the
windows and had waved to us, or they were brandishing
their fists, here the windows are empty. And then, at that
moment, the funeral bell starts to toll. Naturally we take

cover, run with our heads down. Get to the hotel, fast, we're calling to one another in mind as we trundle before us, in our minds, as we move, the curiously twisted human body which lay at our feet a few moments ago. To the hotel, the hotel, we're thinking, in the hope that avoiding the night we will reach morning and hotel at the same time and immediately wake up in the bed that awaits us for the start of a wholly different day, in, if possible, a different place. Farther back in our minds we're also afraid we could be running not to the hotel but into a tourist trap. The notion, repeatedly, that someone might leap out from behind a tree and stab us with a knife, because he thinks the guilt is ours. But we aren't guilty, we insist, and we put our heads down and run. Finally, not joining hands, we're running too fast for that, also we're much too far apart, an insuperable distance, each by himself runs diagonally across the *piazza* outside the hotel, until my wife finally runs into the slaughtering place beneath the pine tree. When she notices where she is, at the slaughtering place, she slows down, stops, and, shoulders up and head down, she tiptoes cautiously around it. Mutely, furtively, not announcing ourselves at the desk, not even rattling the key in the lock, we rush into our ground-floor hotel room. Here, in an instant, I've inserted the key in the lock inside and turned it twice. Then, even before I've laid my cameras and wrist-purse aside, I go to the window and with a loud grinding—for a long time the rusted hooks and latches haven't been used—close the wooden shutters. Why? So as not to have to see the *piazza*, pitch dark, curtained now by silent unexpected clouds, with its trees and benches and slaughtering places submerged. And of course to prevent anyone from looking in on us from outside and seeing how pervasive is the terror we feel in us and around us. For due to the chaos in our minds we're convinced that we share the guilt for the spectacle and that we must pay for it now. What a good thing our little room has only the one window. More, a fragrance comes in from outside, peppermint and other herbs, perhaps thyme. So that less than ten minutes after the end of the spectacle we're in our room in the Hotel Lucia, safe at last, at least for the moment. Only now do I take my cameras off. I push them under the bed. And start, with no idea how we shall spend the night before us, to walk up and down the room, from end to end, from side to side. While my wife, having brushed off her shoes in an instant, never pausing for thought, goes to a corner and stands there, oddly enough with her face to the wall, staying there quietly, sobbing to herself. And when I ask her why she doesn't sit down and try to manhandle her toward the only chair in the room, so that, I'm thinking, she won't be such a nuisance as to collapse in her corner, she refuses to be budged. Since we're still not on speaking terms, I finally set about opening our suitcases and bags and briefcases—strangely out of place here, a heap of prosperity in a corner by the window —and am rummaging through them with no idea what I'm looking for. Yet in our entire luggage, eleven bags, some large, I can't find a thing that might be useful in our situation and help us through the night. Nothing we have with us is the slightest use. The spectacle still haunting us at various angles, at various depths, in that stuffy room we

167

finally pull off our bodies a few sweaty garments and approach, as at a command, though from different sides, the
bed. What a worm-eaten, wooden, dark brown bed, we're
thinking, generations old, in which there has probably
been copulation as well as birth and death! Then when
together we pull the cover back, as if at an agreed signal,
the sheet turns out to be cool, almost clammy. And search-
ing the clammy sheet and clammy pillows for bugs, I do
actually come across one in a fold of the sheet, a repulsive,
black, delicately articulated, longish, thin insect, hardly
visible in the uncertain light, and, what's more, of a kind
unknown to me. My not knowing doesn't mean much, of
course, since any insect is novel and repulsive to a man like
me who comes from an altogether different environment.
Because, during his lifetime, a person like me seldom if
ever meets with insects. Anything, including insects, he's
only read about in books. And now, in a foreign country,
he suddenly comes across such an insect. Yet in a country
like this, in a back country like this, you *have to* expect
that sort of thing. Anyway, the creature is unknown to me
and I decide at once to kill it. And my wife, who is standing for safety's sake behind me, is looking on. Squash it,
is my first thought, before it bites or stings you. And I roll
up my sleeves and wonder: what with? So I look for a wide,
solid object that wouldn't feel a bite or a sting, but can't
find one, either in the room, which is furnished only with a
deep wardrobe, a chair, and a small table, or on my person,
in my pockets. And even if I could find such an object, I
couldn't squash the creature because an insect like that
leaves a stain. Because, out of an insect like that, even

when only slightly injured, a mucous juice trickles, a browish secretion, which would immediately put my wife in a panic. So then panic at the stain in the bed would be added to hysteria about the spectacle. Never, even if I begged on my knees, would my wife sit on a bed soiled with insect juice, yes, she wouldn't go anywhere near such a bed. And that she'd lie down in such a bed and spend the night in it, perhaps even *sleep* in it, is altogether unthinkable. So what am I to do with the creature? How to destroy it? For, small as it is, it can't be ignored, because now that I've made such a fuss my wife has fixed her attention on it. And how attentive she is, how spellbound, studying the creature! How would it be, I'm thinking, if with a resolute movement you simply threw it out of the bed, in which it has obviously been lying for a long time, and on to the floor, then jump on it with your substantial walking shoes, simply crush it? Then dab the flattened remains through a crack in the wooden floorboards, so that she won't tread on it? That's it, I'm thinking, out of the bed and dabbed into the crack! But then, having extracted an old newspaper from one of our suitcases and, paper in hand, having cautiously approached the bed, so as to push the paper quickly under the insect and with one quick flick toss it out of the bed, so as to jump on it, I find that the creature, which, as it now occurs to me, is probably a *scorpion*, has vanished, and even after a lengthy and solicitous search through all the bedclothes it can't be found again. Just at the moment when I'm telling myself it's probably a scorpion, it vanishes inside our bed and can't be found. So that, completely exhausted, we later do sit on the edge of the bed, she, white as a sheet, weeping to herself, and me, calm, I'd like to be calm, I pretend to be calm. And then, as I'd feared, she begins to talk. She asks: Why? Why, she asks. What does she mean, what's she driving at? Whatever it is, the spectacle, her pregnancy, the creature in our bed, our marriage, or Mario, my son, she wants to know, that's certain. But it's also certain that with her in her condition I can't tell her. So I say that I don't understand her, don't know what she means, and even if I did know I can't tell her. True, I say, explanations for everything exist, but when you look at them closely they explain nothing, nothing at all.

Why? she exclaims, why?

Well, I say and wipe my forehead, if you mean the spectacle, then it was an accident. The terrible end of it, I say, spreading my arms, is something nobody could have foreseen. The boy was, I say, an acrobat, and he fell, he'd been meaning to dance up there, he took a false step, I saw it.

You mean, she asks, he didn't jump on purpose?

Jump, I say, why should he?

But, she says, I clearly saw . . .

He was an acrobat and he fell, I exclaim. And put my hand over her mouth, because I suddenly have the impression that someone is eavesdropping, and I say: No more talk now! But although after this we're silent, the room is full of noises, some explainable, others not, noises coming through the shutters or from the ground below. Through the window, magnified by the bare walls, comes the howling of a dog, a noisy animal, looking for something, perhaps a mastiff, or it might be a wolf, prowling over the *piazza.* Perhaps around the slaughtering place, I'm thinking, he's sniffing at it, licking it. (Until recently, so I'd heard, wolves had continually gone into cemeteries here, to dig for fresh corpses. So why not a wolf at the window?) Later then—we've got used to the howling—a stamping from underground, all night until morning, incomprehensible. After some hesitation we tell ourselves: A factory in, or *under,* D.? Haven't we seen everything in the place? Is the tile factory the supervisor told us about not inactive after all? In any case, these noises together with the abrupt, also incomprehensible, also frightening, if not even more frightening, onsets of silence, saw to it that toward midnight my wife, red-eyed and with her face swollen, in spite of her fear and disgust long since prostrate on the disheveled, rummaged-through, and scorpion-inhabited bed, simply tumbles into the bed. Yes, at a certain point during the night—I'm by then standing at the window, but not looking out, I can't, because of the shutters—she simply sinks into the bed behind me, so that now I face the manifold terrors of the night alone. It was then that I took the writing paper out of my briefcase, laid it on the spindly-legged table, moved the table cautiously under the feeble ceiling light, and of course not on the table, it's much too wobbly, but on my knees, which I've crossed, wrote amid the noises penetrating my body to the bone a letter to my wife stretched out behind me. I wanted to tell her the *truth* about us, finally, without bogging down in the details. But since I can't of course tell her the *whole truth* about us—at least not in a single night, not in the village of D., not in a single letter, while putting myself behind me, open-mouthed, sweat on my brow—what part of the truth will you write to her then, I'm wondering. If she just knew, I'm thinking, how very far away from her you are, emotionally. And then I write to her that I'd wanted for a long time to tell her the truth, no matter what part of it, but that I'd never had the courage, "and that is why I'm telling you in writing what follows, unaffected by your usual pat answers." No, you can't write the bit about "pat answers," I'm thinking, and I crumple the sheet of paper up, take a fresh one, and write: Dear Maria, this letter will surprise you, since for three weeks we've been on vacation together and have had time enough to talk about everything. I mean our marriage, of course, which as we both know has gone wrong recently. Why, although I never left you in any doubt as to my intentions and desires, did you even let yourself have a child by me, I write. I *don't want* the child, I simply couldn't stand this child and I'd— I write, my handwriting horrible, contorted like my position, physical and emotional, it's hardly legible, I hardly recognize it as my own, I can't possibly expect her to read it, or the contents of it, I tell myself. No, you must destroy it at once, I'm thinking, and I do destroy the second sheet too, crumple it up and take a fresh one, the third. Dear Maria, I write, near enough, and I decide simply to write now everything that's passing through my mind, together with the way it's doing so. And that's how I did write. Why did you move my sofa from my workroom last April and put it in the living room, when I'd expressly said that you shouldn't? And that's only one example. So that you've gradually managed to turn my house, where I should supposedly have good feelings, into a place of misery for me, uninhabitable. Perhaps you think, I write, that I don't notice your *offenses,* but you're wrong. No, the word *offenses* is too strong, I'm thinking, and I'm about to crumple this sheet too, or at least cross out the last sentence, but I don't cross it out, nor do I crumple up the sheet, I just go on writing. And I do so because at the moment I'm thinking that given our temperaments, hers and mine, things couldn't help going rapidly the way they've gone. But this, I continue, could be overcome. Because until now—and this was a mistake—instead of discussing our problems, "which exist, I don't dispute it," each of us has been swallowing his problems. There are devilish ways, I write, in which man opposes woman, woman opposes man, and that's true for us as well. On the other hand, I write, I'm of course infinitely grateful to you for taking such good care of our child, who is quite a stranger to me, unfortunately. If she grows up to be a good person, it's you she'll have to thank, you alone. And if, as I admit, I've had a relationship with another person—it was always fleeting, always hurry-hurry—I've carefully kept it from you, on purpose, I write. But not so as to deceive you, but because I didn't want to burden you or upset you with it. Also these things belong to the past and are finished and done with. The woman, I go on writing, was called Barbara, in case you don't already know. Fine, that's what I'll write, so that's what I wrote. And because I'm exhausted from the day's events and from our trip itself and haven't many ideas in my head for more things to write to her, the gaps between spates of writing have been getting longer, I've had my head in my hands often, wondering what else to write. So that I then wrote compulsively what I never should have done. For instance, that in our case it was a mistake to get married at all. But in obliging us to get married when we did, through your own default, I write, you weren't doing yourself a favor. No, I'm thinking, you really can't write that, *not that,* and I'm about to cross out the sentence, but I don't cross it out, I go on writing. And at the same time I'm listening to the night noises, taking them apart and putting them together again, while riffling with my left thumb the writing paper in front of me. It's horrible, a decision to part like this, I'm thinking, atrocious, a letter like this. Later I stand up, take off my shoes, stretch my limbs and walk around barefoot, so as not to wake her up. And imagine myself leaving the hotel a free man, with the luggage, while in reality I can't leave the hotel, least of all with the luggage. And just when midnight is approaching, or already past, but still nothing has happened—I'm writing down almost illegibly the word *reconciliation,* just because it's passing through my mind— my wife starts to groan, she may be awake, or dreaming. I stand up and walk to the bed. She's lying uncovered, breathing heavily, sweat on her shoulders in the sheeted kip, where the insect had been, and on her left side, turned toward me, with her legs drawn up, her hands to her stomach. And as I sit down on the edge of the bed I feel how warm her body is. Your wife, I'm thinking, and I consider her carefully dyed, no, toned hair, which to the touch is so lifeless, despite all the care it receives, and which has unfortunately such an indifferent smell, too. And then, in the murky light, one leg crossed over the other, to the rhythm of the incomprehensible stamping, I suddenly can't help thinking of Mimiddu, but *before* he died. So I'm thinking of his hair, ribs, calves, teeth, *his* smile, et cetera. How terrible to die and be buried in a place like D., I'm thinking. But I don't think of his dying so soon— and of how he died—that's something I brush aside, and can brush aside. As if he'd never lain face down, that's how I'm thinking of him, I unbutton my shirt. What a good-looking boy! I don't want to think of him anymore, and so I don't. But then, I don't know why, I'm thinking of the other boy, by the other tower, the one of twenty years ago, the one that might have been a Norman tower. And how this boy, his shirt open to his navel, comes toward me under the tower and smilingly pushes his strong brown thumb first into his own mouth, then into mine. Damn it, I'm thinking, damn it! In contrast—my poor pale wife, always ready for it, who, life-size, is breathing on my knee, my left knee. Damn it, I'm thinking, damn it! And I breathe more deeply, to take in more of the dull, lifeless air of this night. Then I pull her closer. Her limp body, her shoulders with their markings, her round knee. Grudgingly she opens her eyes, emerges from her sleep. I don't say anything, take her head, and lay it in my lap. She's rigid as ever, my blond-toned wife, no longer quite fresh, no longer so very young. I unbutton myself. Hold me, I say, put your hand here.

No, she says, leave me alone.

But I hold her tight. I point to her blouse. Undo the buttons, I say, go on, undo them.

Please, she says, don't touch me. And every time I move her mouth, throat, breasts into position she shifts them away from me. No, she says, I don't want to.

Then I take hold of her by force and draw her to me and press her head between my thighs. There, I say, you know what I want. And remind her that until now I've always been the stronger of us. Then comes my crude grappling with her head, mouth, breasts. But I make up for it all when I brush my forefinger softly over her lips.

Do it now, I say.

No, she says, not now. I can't. I don't want to. You must be crazy.

Then hold it, at least touch it, I say.

No, she says, there's no point.

Do it, I say, please do it.

You're killing me, don't you realize? Don't you see? she says.

Yes, I say, keep on doing it. There, I say, put your hand there. Yes, that's it, I say.

You swine, she says, you swine.

You know, I say, after she's been doing it for a while, I once used to know boys like the one today. You can ask me about it, if you like.

It doesn't interest me who you knew, she says. I don't want to know.

All the same, I say, ask me about it.

No, she says.

Ask me, I say, ask.

All right, she says, if it's necessary.

176

Yes, I say, it's necessary.

Were there many? she asks. But don't touch me, she says.

All right if I just put my hand there, just there, I ask. And then, after a while: No, actually there weren't many.

No, she says, don't put your hand there.

Don't stop, I say. And ask me.

What should I ask?

About them, I say.

How did you do it with them, she asks.

The last time was about twelve years ago, I say, before you knew me. It must have been somewhere near here, there was a tower, too, you know. I hoped I'd found it again when that man talked about it, but it wasn't the same tower after all. You know, I say, that time, twelve years ago, it almost made me die.

You swine, she says, you swine.

Every time, I say, it almost made me die.

You swine, she says, don't touch me.

All right, I say, but go on asking. Go on asking, I yell.

Did you kiss them, your little baby swine, she asks.

Yes, I say. And made them kiss me.

You swine, she says, you swine.

Ask some more, I say.

Did you touch them, she asks.

Yes, I say, yes, yes.

You swine, she says, you swine.

Keep on doing it, I say. Ask where.

Where, she asks, you old swine.

In the country, I say, beneath the olive trees. Somewhere

not far from here. In the shadow of the great wheels of the ox cart.

And there, she asks, did you touch them there, too. And she touches me.

Yes, I say, yes, there.

And there too, she asks, did you touch them there. And she touches me.

Yes, I say, there too.

Oh, she says, Oh.

Don't stop, I say.

Don't put your hand there, she says.

I only want, I say, very gently to . . .

No, she says, don't ever put your hand there again.

Don't you want to know what I did with them, I ask.

I don't care what you did with them, she says.

But ask, I say, please ask.

What did you do with them, she asks, but don't put your hand on me.

Does it hurt, I ask.

That's none of your business, she says.

Ask me first if I *really* did it, I ask, you know who with.

I don't care if you did it or who with, she says. After today I don't care about anything at all.

But ask me, all the same, I say.

Did you do it, she asks.

Yes, I say. Ask me how often.

How often, she asks.

Twelve times, I say, twelve times.

With several, she asks, or all the times with one?

With several, I say, but mostly with one.

You swine, she says, you swine.

And now ask me, I say, if I really did . . . Or only had fantasies.

Did you really do it, she asks.

Yes, I say, yes, yes, yes. If you want, I can tell you all about it, the details. I haven't forgotten anything, I say, it's all there still. Shall I tell you.

No, she says.

Don't stop, I say, don't stop now.

Do you often think of them, she asks.

Yes, fairly often, I say. And you, I say, you? Tell me what you're always thinking of.

I don't know, she says, I haven't done anything. I haven't got anything to think about.

Don't cry now, I say, at least not so loud. People can hear everything. Just don't stop.

I can't go on.

What's wrong, I ask, are you sick?

Yes, she says, I'm sick.

What's the matter, I ask.

Everything, I'm just sick, that's all.

Why, I ask, because of me?

Yes, she says, also because of you.

Because of what I told you?

Yes, she says, because of that as well.

Because of the way I am with you, I ask.

Yes, she says, because of the way you are. Don't put your hand there, she says.

If you don't want to, I say, you needn't.

All right, she says, I'll stop now. I don't want to, never did.

So what, I say. Just a bit more.

And then, she says, how did you talk them into it? Did you threaten them, too? Did you force them, too? Because you were stronger?

No, I say, not them.

But how, she asks.

With money, I say.

Always with money, she asks.

Yes, I say, always with money, but that's quite natural. And you, haven't you ever done it?

Done what?

Taken money, I ask.

No, she says, never.

More, I say, don't stop now.

Don't touch me, she says, don't ever touch me again.

You look terrible, I say.

How do you mean, terrible? she asks.

As if you were sick, I say. With fever.

So I'm sick then, she says, so I'll die.

Maria, I say, don't say that.

Don't touch me, she says, don't touch me.

And because she usually never does it when she's sick, I still ask: Will you do it even if you're sick? And then, through all the sweat: Soon now, don't stop, soon, don't stop now! And when she has finished and is sitting in the bed, quivering a little, her body slightly bent, and wants to say something, she can't say it. She can't breathe properly. I pass my hand over her forehead and it really is a bit warm. And I see her longish, slightly pointed fingernails, always a delicate rose color, but now quite white. While, around her eyes, there is fear in dark rings . . . Yes, perhaps she has a fever. I push her head away from me, lift it from my lap and stretch out my legs and ask her how she feels, but she doesn't answer. So she doesn't feel well, I'm thinking. And that I shouldn't have made any claims on her in her condition, shouldn't have asked anything of her this night.

Is there something you want to tell me, I ask.

But there isn't. Or perhaps there is, and she can't tell it. And again I blame the air, which is really very stale, very thick, and there's not enough of it in this low-ceilinged, remarkably oppressive room tonight. And since she's sobbing, making little sounds, even little pipings, I put my arm around her shoulder and say: keep your chin up, Maria! And that everything will get better once we've left this room and this village of D. Everything as it was before, I'm about to say, but I don't. And I beg her to be calm now and not always be thinking of the atrocious accident, which, thank God, doesn't affect us personally and is actually no concern of ours at all.

Quick now, forget it, I exclaim, and clap my hands.

She looks at me big-eyed and nods, too, but she isn't listening and she doesn't forget the accident, either, forgets nothing, but, as I realize more and more clearly, is thinking about it and about everything else too with more and more abandon. Meanwhile with a cupped hand I'm fanning air across her shoulders, there isn't much of it, so that she'll finally be able to talk and dredge up from herself the thing that's tormenting her. But, as I see, it isn't the lack of air, her condition is what's stopping her from speaking, expressing herself. And then suddenly, after turning as far away from me as she can, her eyes closed, in the deep bed, where the creature also is, which I now realize, I'd entirely forgotten, and with her legs drawn up as far as they'll go, pushing her terror away from her as resolutely as she can: It's the other thing, she says, holding her wet batiste handkerchief pressed in a tiny ball to her mouth, *my* thing, she says, you needn't worry about it anymore.

In my obtuseness, doltishness, folly, exhaustion, I ask her: What do you mean?

The thing you were so afraid of, she says, and turns still farther away. The child. I'm bleeding now, she says, don't touch me.

15

And she has me stand up, after we've sat side by side on the excessively low bed in silence for several minutes buried in fundamentally different, even diametrically opposite feelings and thoughts, and go into a corner, because, as she says, she now wants to *freshen* up. Freshen up, good then, I'm thinking. No, she doesn't want any help from me, no, go away, go away, go away, she shrieks. And then because I don't obey at once she even pushes me off the bed. Slowly, doing up my belt, I get to my feet, slip into my shoes, stamp my feet into them. And walk, after pacing through the room once more, to the door. And for a long time I stand, in the same corner, even in the same posture as hers, the corner into which she'd gone, to sob, when she entered the room. And I can hear her standing up from the bed behind me and going to her suitcases, stooping, opening them. Don't turn around, she says. And keeping my face to the wall I can hear her going back to the bed, taking something off, putting something on, slowly, dispiritedly, reluctantly.

Don't turn around, she keeps saying, do you hear, don't turn around.

She's bleeding, I'm thinking, how strange! Well, I'm thinking, as I study the wall, particularly stained at this point, at which she sobbed for such a long time, the worry's over. And tell myself it was the shock, she owes the bleeding to the shock. Without the shock, I'm sure now, she'd still be pregnant. And that probably right after our arrival at the tower, I figure, thus even before she bit the supervisor's hand, she'd felt that a shock was going to strike her any moment and release the drop of menstrual blood. Perhaps, I'm thinking, *while* she was biting him, perhaps she bit him *because* of it. Yes, I tell myself, as I study the wall, first the fear, then the vomiting, then the shock. And now the blood, I'm thinking. Because with her living such a sheltered life she simply wasn't prepared for a spectacle like that. Because she simply never had anticipated that such a spectacle could be conceived of and then carried out, in our day and age, as it were on our doorstep. And even now, at this moment, D. is not yet behind us. For you haven't seen the last of the supervisor, I'm thinking, he'll show up again. On the other hand, I can now forget all the arguments I'd gathered against her pregnancy and the child. The matter has been settled of its own accord, that is, according to nature, by spontaneous discharge. That settles also the letter you wrote her, but it mustn't fall into her hands, you can destroy it, no, you *must* destroy it. And I decide that as soon as possible, thus as soon as she calls me from the corner, to go to the table, to crumple up the letter I've hidden under the writing paper, and, not explaining anything, to put it in my pocket. And when I can, when she's not looking, to tear it into a thousand pieces. And drop the pieces into a toilet and flush them away, I'm thinking. Or scatter them to the winds out of the window of the moving car.

When she does call me from my corner I'm nevertheless a bit startled by the bloody garment which my wife, usually tact, no, prudery itself in such matters, has left in the middle of the bed, probably to punish me. As a souvenir of what you've done to me, this garment will lie this night between us, that's what she'll have thought, and so she has laid it on the bed. I look at the garment for a long time, but say nothing, and walk a few times up and down by the bed, hoping she could have left it there by an oversight, not drawing her attention to it or complaining about it or picking it up and stowing it in her suitcase. Anyway she seems to be bleeding a great deal. There's even a patch in the bedclothes, which she also hasn't covered up. Generally, throughout this night, most of all during the second half of it, because of the bolted shutters, there's a bad smell in the room. Nothing much else happens and not a word more is said. Yes, not even any remarks are made, on her part or mine, but everything remains unsaid between us, she on her bed, me on my chair. Only as morning is announcing itself with the first gray light in the window gap and the light is coming through the chinks, and in hastily donned clothes—it has become cool—and with our shoes laced we're sitting speechless opposite one another in the twilight like two pallid nocturnal animals, only then can we hear something. Not the stamping from below, and not the howling of the dog—those sounds we now take for granted—but a shuffling that we think at first is an illusion we ourselves are projecting, but it turns out to be a shuffling outside, probably moving past the hotel. Somebody slowly walking by the hotel wall making a noise as if he were dragging a broom behind him. My wife, colorless, as one might imagine, with hollow cheeks, wearing a sort of horse blanket which she has discovered in the depths of the wardrobe and dragged out and thrown over her shoulders, doesn't let me know that she can hear it, or perhaps she actually doesn't hear it, or doesn't *want* to, thinking it will go away if she pays no attention to it, but instead the shuffling comes closer. Then, when it is so close that she *must* hear it, she sort of freezes.

Listen, she whispers. And: Switch the light off! And: What is it? she asks.

Well, I say and unhurriedly stand up and switch off the light, so that we're in the dark again. And so as to indicate to her, even without speaking, that the shuffling can't mean any harm, so as to defuse it for her, as it were, I even yawn. Well, I say again, making a clumsy attempt, which she at once nips in the bud, to show her some tenderness: Who might it be now?

The *meccanico*, bringing the car? she asks, hopefully.

Possibly, I say, although I know better, for I've long, no, always known that we won't elude the supervisor so easily and leave D. without bumping into him again. From whom we'd escaped into the *vicoli*, after the spectacle, and after she'd bent double and bolted away with a howl so loud that it echoed and I had followed her calling Maria! Maria! And then it occurs to me that I'd heard the shuffling occasionally during the night, when she'd been asleep and I'd been brooding over the now superfluous letter, but I hadn't investigated the matter, thinking it was only an illusion. So then it hadn't been an illusion after all and the supervisor had probably been wandering around the hotel at night, only with more restraint and more quietly, and he, like us, and with the same fervor as us, had been hoping for first light to dawn, for morning. And now that first light has dawned he's shuffling more audibly around our hotel. How awkward, I'm thinking. And then, a bit later, perhaps around five, with her knees pressed tightly together, my wife is sitting up in the bed from which she can't remove the blood, because there's no water in the room, and the bed with the dark stain gradually reddening in the dawn light now looks horribly as if something had been killed in it, something slaughtered. Anyway: around five, while I'm walking softly back and forth before my wife and quietly telling her, so as to calm her down, the story of how we're driving home and how we've put the island behind us and are already at the ferry, and as I'm placing my hand, every so often, though fleetingly, on her cheek, we can hear the supervisor's footsteps quite clearly. I can't see him through the chinks in the shutter, but then, clearly audible, he walks through the front door into the hotel.

You hear? she whispers. And after a while, when the supervisor, announcing himself, but also perhaps threatening, has cleared his throat a few times in the hotel corridor, she again says: You hear? Now!

Well, I say and shrug my shoulders, not knowing if she sees that I do so. So what? I ask, so what?

No, she says, craning her neck and listening toward the door, it's not the *meccanico.*

No, I say, as casually as I can. And why, I ask, acting all innocence, why shouldn't it be the *meccanico?*

No, not the *meccanico,* she says softly and, after listening briefly once more toward the door and then for a longer time listening inside herself, she shakes her head. And asks if it's *him.*

Him? I ask.

You know who, she says.

Well, I say, pulling myself up to my full height before her, if it's not the *meccanico,* then it might be. And that he'd probably come to say good-bye to us.

Good-bye, she exclaims.

Yes, I say. All this night now almost past I've been generally lying and sitting, also standing, with or without something to lean against, everywhere else in the room, so now I go once more to the window, which is still closed, and look, I don't know for how long, through the chinks, without seeing much. Slowly the twilight disengages the umbrella pine's contours, which I've remembered, also the firs and cypresses outside are resurrected, just the same as they'd been in my mind. A classic landscape, an incomparable landscape, but D., I'm thinking, what a hole! And then when I catch sight of myself reflected in the window-pane—I'd been looking through myself for as long as I could—I hardly recognize myself at first. Strange, I think, so that's how you look after a single sleepless night, after a single spectacle of that kind. And I look at myself, startled, for a long time, I study myself with horror. And while I'm expressing once more to my wife, who is sitting behind me, how much I'd like to have spared her this stay in D., the shuffling and scraping starts afresh and I realize that the supervisor is standing now outside our ill-fitting door. At once I hold my breath and walk over to my wife, and I immediately imagine him—as I'm sure my wife does —precisely as he is standing with his legs apart outside the door, in mourning clothes, padded, wearing a grubby shirt that's bursting out all over him. And that he's quite certain, in his round skull, that we're on the other side of the door and imagining him, waiting for him. Perhaps he can even hear us breathing. (Although both my wife and I are breathing only very little, almost not at all, during these moments.) What does he want, we're both thinking, each to himself, while outside, so as to scare us, there's a new spate of scraping. And then, with the points of claws, from the top to the bottom, thus doglike, a slight scratching at our door, then horizontally, between the doorposts. Standing upright in front of my wife, in response to her un-spoken request, I draw her head to me and for a long time I don't respond, in hope that the scratching will stop and he'll think the room is empty and we've left, and that he'll go away too, which doesn't however happen, but he goes on scratching. So that, while stroking her blond-toned hair, to calm my wife, I break my silence and ask in a loud voice who's there.

He, simultaneously clearing his throat and scraping and scratching: It's me, Herr Hans, who do you think?

So then of course I reply that we don't want to see anyone, least of all him. We're tired, have hardly slept, are still in bed. Later perhaps, I exclaim.

But the supervisor, as on his first appearance, doesn't let up and he exclaims in reply that he must talk to us *now and at once.*

Talk then, but only that, I exclaim, and I walk to the door.

Yes, talk, only talk, he exclaims.

What about, I ask and put my ear to the door.

Because there's a question, he exclaims.

Unnecessary, I exclaim, quite unnecessary.

Well then, he exclaims, some news.

Who from, I ask.

A suggestion, he says.

So early, I exclaim, my ear to the door.

Yes, so early, he says.

So does it have to be now, I ask.

Yes, he says, now.

Better open up, he knows we're here, I say softly to my wife, and have the feeling, even then, that he can understand every word.

No, she exclaims, no, never! And then she even leaps out of the bed and stands at the door with her arms outspread. And she even wants—it's understandable, but impossible —to barricade the door against the supervisor, to move the wobbly table, the deep wardrobe, yes, most of all the low but wide bed up against the door.

So you want to make a fool of yourself in a foreign country? I exclaim. And I tell her quite categorically that, whoever is at the door, be it the devil himself, the furniture stays where it is. And that we couldn't deny him a chance to *speak his mind,* even if I didn't know what he'd talk about, I say, for the accident did happen, after all. And that we couldn't possibly deny him the chance. For if we want to get out of this room and out of D., I whisper, more or less, it will have to be through *this* door, and, if he keeps on standing outside, we'll have to go past him, sooner or later. And after pulling the cameras and wrist-purse out from under the bed and having hung them around me, and, just in case, having taken the clasp knife out of the hamper and put it into my trouser pocket, the right-hand one, and once my wife, now fully dressed, her blouse buttoned to the neck, the garment stuffed into a suitcase, the bloodstain covered with a pillow, has settled herself on a chair, with clenched teeth and bolt upright, I walk to the door and turn—having taken two or three deep breaths—the key in the lock. And I open the door with my foot, not my hands, just to show the supervisor at once how utterly I despise him, giving it a kick, and I gesture to him wordlessly—I'll be saying nothing for a time—into our room. The supervisor, still shadowy in the corridor, has hardly crossed the threshold when he resumes the familiar contours and consolidates himself before our eyes, to become the familiar dense shape. We also soon adjust to his face, which is a bit more haggard, a bit more pale, and has a thick stubble far down the neck. Yes, indeed, that's his double chin, to be sure, that's his mustache. And there's his theatricality, the oiliness. No trace on him of any deep and visible, even tragic change worked by the terrible spectacle. But his suit, we see, is even more rumpled and the hairdo piled up on his skull is in even greater disarray, and the wine red shoes, because he has first led us through D. and then pursued us through D., are even filthier than they were yesterday. He isn't wearing a sash. And then, the moment he comes in, the perverse ritual of joy and cordiality that he unwinds around us. First the arms are spread, to signify an embrace, but I wave him away before he can come any closer.

No, I exclaim.

No, he asks.

No, I exclaim.

All right, no, he says and lowers his arms. Well, he says, later perhaps. And next he goes over to my wife and forgets her bite and makes a deep bow to her and wants to take her hand and kiss it, but I intervene and with a single motion of my right hand nail him to the spot.

No, I say.

Not that either, he asks.

No, I say, not that either.

And why not, he asks and looks up at me askance.

Because we don't need it, I say. And at the same time with my left hand I throw (thinking: we need light, light) the shutters open. And draw myself up, since it's suddenly bright in the room and in an instant the room looks as shabby and uninhabitable as it always was, to face the supervisor head-on, while he, cut short in speech and motion, stands there speechless, with his cane between his legs. All right, I'm thinking, and now? It's obvious that sometime this morning—I hope the car arrives soon —we'll have to talk about the spectacle. And that when we do I'll have to express to him our terror, horror, abhorrence, et cetera, and finally strike my fist on the table or on the windowsill, too. The question is: now or later? And *how* am I to formulate our abhorrence, convey our horror. Should I do it loudly and excitedly and abruptly, coming down on him like a ton of bricks, or urgently and quietly, coming up at him from underneath, with an undertone of entreaty? To shout or not to shout? No, I'm thinking, you can't shout, because there may still be other guests in the hotel, for even if it's daylight now outside, it's probably still bedtime for people here. Well then, I say, and stamp my foot a little, the right foot.

If you don't mind, the supervisor says, bowing slightly.

Go on, I say, and tap my foot.

We lost track of each other, he says, yesterday.

Lost track, I exclaim and give a laugh.

Yes, he says, last night.

Do you hear that? We lost track of each other last night, I exclaim, trying to catch my wife's eye, but she's looking at the floor.

Yes, he says, at the tower, in the crowd.

No, my dear sir, we didn't *lose track* of each other, as you express it, I exclaim, standing more upright, we escaped.

Because we didn't want to see anybody anymore, I say, we couldn't.

Aha, he says.

And now imagine our astonishment, I say and spread my arms, the person we escaped from is suddenly here again. Unnecessary, I exclaim, utterly unnecessary.

Aha, he says, aha. And after a while, laying a finger along his nose: Who? he asks.

What? I ask.

Who, he asks, is unnecessary?

The person, I say, who comes knocking at our door so early in the morning.

You mean, he says, during the time when everybody is asleep?

Yes, I say.

So then, he asks, you mean me.

The person who comes knocking so early should know that himself, I exclaim, sharply, speaking to the side and into the room.

He doesn't say anything. He seems to be thinking.

So you've been waiting for me, he asks, after a while.

What makes you think that, I exclaim. What an idea. And so early, too. And I stamp my feet.

So then, he says and pulls his jacket tighter, you were *not* waiting for me?

Yes, of course we were, I say.

Aha, he says.

But whether or not we were waiting for you isn't the question at all, I exclaim, the question is . . .

Naturally, he says and falls silent.

No, I'm thinking, this isn't the right way, you've started wrong. And what, I ask myself, are you doing wrong? Your sentences, I'm thinking, are too short! With such short, terse sentences, however menacingly you speak them, you'll never get through to a supervisor such as this. You must make up much longer, harder sentences, ones that are more real, and coil them, as it were, around his neck. And then pull, I'm thinking. And draw breath at the word *pulling*, for since I opened the shutters there's not only much more light, but also much more air in the room. And I set about composing a long, as it were inescapable sentence, containing all our terror and horror, but now the past night, which I'd spent without sleep, though I'd forgotten this, is taking its toll—and I can't speak the sentence. I can't even begin it. For heaven's sake, you're not succumbing to your weakness, are you, I'm thinking. Do it now, start the sentence! But even while I'm thinking this, I've succumbed. The fact is, I'm no longer used to passing a night without sleep. And we know already that for me physical details suppress all feelings, even feelings of abhorrence and outrage. So that due to fatigue and weakness I've suddenly become incapable of uttering the least protest, of asking for the least explanation, and all I can do is give a loud yawn and so introduce into the bright but shabby room a huge moral vacuum. And I almost resent the silence to which my look has just reduced the supervisor. Why then doesn't *he* say something? Eventually, I give up the idea of insisting that he explain the spectacle. Also in the presence of my wife, who believes it was an *accident*, I can't mention a leap. Also the idea that I might reprove him for *endangering a young human life*—at least he sent him up the tower, made him dance at the top—and then take him by the shoulders, turn him around in the room and push him out through the ill-fitting door—I give that idea up too. I do something altogether different. What I do is drag, as if he weren't there at all—and I've got to do something—the biggest and heaviest of our suitcases out of its corner and knock on it a few times and tighten its leather strap and haul the suitcase just past the feet of the supervisor, who's in my way, to the door. And then, when I've examined every single suitcase and bag and briefcase, everything that was piled up by the window, and when I've hauled it all past the supervisor's feet to the door and have all this time said nothing at all, I quietly say, from the window, where I've positioned myself, looking up at the pine tree, but with an empty look: Something I wanted to ask you, since you've come from outside—did you by any chance meet with the *meccanico?* Or did you happen to see our car, which has been repaired now and should be here any moment.

But the supervisor hasn't seen either of them, and I say: Well, I didn't expect that you would have, but you might have.

No, the supervisor says, I haven't seen anything and I think your car won't be here for a long time, but there's something I want to explain to you now.

Explain? I exclaim and act astonished. I hope this explanation won't take long, I exclaim, because, as you see—

and I point to the suitcases—we want to leave, very early,
in fact right away.
But you can't, the supervisor says, not right away.
What do you mean? I say and toss my head, and who's
going to stop us?
The car, he says, isn't here yet.
Don't you worry, I say, the car will be here.
If you say so, the supervisor says. But if I could perhaps
give my explanation in the meantime, actually it's a
question.
Be quick about it, I say.
Well then, the supervisor says, if you don't mind. And
first he bows to my wife, then to me, and, with the cane
between his legs, is about to launch into one of those long
sentences of which I'm not capable, due to my weakness,
but I've changed my mind and am *against* the explanation, short or long. And I exclaim, my right hand in my
pocket where the knife is, interrupting his bow: No, no
explanation, no.
And why not, he asks, looking at me in amazement.
Because I've changed my mind, I say.
And might I ask a question, he asks.
No, I say, no questions either. And I walk across the whole
room, with its echoes from underneath, to my wife, who
is sitting there upright and dry-eyed, and position myself
behind her, hands on her shoulders, as if at this moment
we were sitting for a matutinal double portrait. A strange,
profoundly unbelievable, and ridiculous pose, as I'm willing to admit. And I'm thinking: Mimiddu didn't fall,

Mimiddu jumped! And whether he fell or jumped, I want to hear no more of it. But precisely because I don't want to hear any more of it, I'm at once watching the spectacle again in my thoughts, if only in them, I'm in the natural grandstand, and the boy, with a lively and energetic movement, as if he were laughing about something, hops lightly on to the guard wall, and any moment now he's going to jump for us. To be lying thereafter, preceded by his cry, in midair, with nothing to hold on to, and—strangely twisted limbs—one can't see the wound that killed him . . . All of this I imagine, with my hands on Maria's shoulders. As if I'd traveled to the south not for pleasure but for torment. Until with two or three thrusts of my arms, first to the right, then to the left, I manage to repulse my memories and push them, with fingers outspread, into the window corner where until now the luggage has been. Outside, signaling the passage of time, the new day is rapidly arriving. And why doesn't the car arrive? Eventually, after I've stood around for I don't know how long, with a gloomy face and arms hanging at my sides, I tell myself: Get it over with! And that's the way it works. I put my hands in my pockets to have them out of the way, and leaning forward on the tips of my toes I exclaim, with silences interspersed: Well now! Well now! Well now! And I'm meaning, in spite of fatigue, weakness, limpness, emptiness, et cetera, finally to tell the supervisor how outraged, how aghast I am at the "accident," as I propose to say, but how? Like anyone who reads his daily paper, I constantly have occasion to be transfixed and dumbfounded by all sorts of catastrophes, bestialities, inhumanities, because, more and more often, things I can't accommodate are rushing into me. Right, so I'm dumbfounded, right, I'm transfixed with horror. I sit there, my eyes are shut, the paper is on the floor, while the catastrophes have long since gone into my head, but what can I do? With those catastrophes in my head, I haven't for years been able to say anything about them, I've simply carried them around with me in silence. As for believing that any outcry can be effectual, I just don't go along with that anymore. Which is why I make no outcry now, either, and instead only say, several times, helplessly: A child, a child, a child! And because the man doesn't understand me: He fell, I exclaim, he fell from the tower! What were you saying to the boy, I eventually exclaim, very loud, but I can't suppress another yawn, and I continue more quietly, when you were standing on the ladder? Why, I ask, were you knocking so hard on the tower yesterday? You were knocking on the tower, I ask, weren't you?

Yes, he says and nods, that's right.

And you spoke with the boy from the ladder?

Yes, he says, we had a talk, too.

Well, I say and yawn again and forget my question and exclaim instead once more: A child, a child, a child! From hereabouts, I suppose? I ask.

Yes, he says, from hereabouts.

Whose family you presumably know, I ask.

I do know the family, he says.

Lots of children, I suppose?

Yes, he says, lots.

And poor, I ask.

Yes, he says.

Do you hear that, Maria, I say, there are too many children here. So the small ones, almost as soon as they can walk, are taught all kinds of tricks. Like dancing on the top of an old tower, on the guard wall, I exclaim. Just to bring some money home, I suppose, I ask.

Yes, he says, it's for money.

Do you hear that, I say to her. It's exactly as I thought. The boy was trained as an acrobat, a sort of artist.

I find you both disgusting, she says, each as disgusting as the other.

Maria, I exclaim.

Yes, the supervisor says, his right hand on his member. And now he's dead. And then, after hesitating a while: Were we—he looks at his fingernails—satisfied with the spectacle?

How do you mean, I ask.

Well, he says, was the extraordinary experience successfully conveyed?

Experience, I exclaim, listen now! How can we be satisfied when such a ghastly accident . . .

So you're not satisfied, he exclaims, and he brings out his cigarettes.

But surely, I exclaim, you don't mean to say . . . And I'm thinking: It's not possible! Surely he won't tell us, in the presence of your wife, in her condition, that the boy didn't fall but, well . . . jumped? Since my wife is sitting on her chair between us I can't even shush him up, but I do wink at him. And say: An accident, yes, an accident.

But it wasn't an accident at all, he exclaims and puts a cigarette between his lips.

Yes, yes, it was, I say and now I'm blinking at him too. An accident, the kind that does happen and can't be avoided. Look at my wife here, I exclaim, see how badly the accident affected her. So let's talk, I say, about something different.

Why, he says and lights his cigarette.

So you mean, I say, and I make a longish pause, so that the stillness of the room can pass across and settle on the truth we've been pushing aside and hushing up, but which is erupting now and can't any longer be kept secret. That the boy, I say, I mean Mimiddu, I mean, so he hadn't intended to dance? I say.

No, the supervisor says and takes a drag on his cigarette, he never intended to dance. He can't have, he never learned how. He never learned anything at all, he exclaims and draws and puffs on his cigarette.

So then, I say, *if* what you say . . . then he must have . . .

Yes, he says, it's true what I'm saying.

Not have slipped, I say, not have just fallen at all.

No, the supervisor says peevishly and immediately he has put his hand, after tapping the cigarette ash off around the room, on his member again, he didn't slip, didn't fall.

So then, I exclaim, he must have jumped?

Correct, he darkly exclaims, he jumped.

So he jumped, I say and look down at my wife, to see how she's taking it, but her eyes are closed, her breathing inaudible, her face expressionless. And she won't be saying anything, either, because, to hold back the scream that's always possible with her, she has put her handkerchief in her mouth and is chewing on it. In the first light of day—it'll certainly be a classically beautiful day—she has put the white batiste handkerchief I bought for her in Bruges between her teeth and she's biting on it, hard.

Maria, I exclaim, what's this you're doing?

For there's no mistake: My wife, on this beautiful morning, is *eating* her handkerchief. She knew actually all along, like everyone else in the grandstand—except that she didn't want to know it—that the boy didn't fall but, forced or persuaded for some inconceivably perverse end, deliberately, and for us, so that we should see him doing so, had jumped from the tower. For mercy's sake, she has been telling herself, let it be that he fell, so I won't have to think of it anymore. And now that the supervisor has destroyed this thought too, she's eating, so help me God, in response to some signal inside her head, her lace handkerchief. Maria, I exclaim, your handkerchief.

And I stand there, unable to decide what to do. Why doesn't the supervisor go away, why doesn't he leave us in peace? When one considers that at this time yesterday we didn't even know the man, had no idea of his existence! And even before that, too, when he was busy in Frankfurt. How seldom do we go to Frankfurt, with good reason, apparently! And now? What more does he want from us, why doesn't he leave us in peace? Instead of starting all over again and asking us again—it's really as if he had our heads against a grindstone—whether, yes or no, we'd been satisfied with the spectacle. Jumped, jumped, I exclaim and spread my arms out. Yes, he says, for you. But, I exclaim, did we ever expect, ever imagine . . . Possibly, I admit, that someone else, perhaps . . . But why, I exclaim, why?

Because of the contract, he says and smokes.

So, I say, there was a contract with the boy?

With his family, he says. And holding the cigarette between his lips he gropes in his pocket and pulls out a sheet of paper and tries to press into my hand the contract which, as I see, has been signed by one of the two parties, thus probably the family, with three crosses, and which is certainly against this country's laws.

Here, he says. And with the cigarette drooping from his lips. Why don't you look at it?

No, stop it, I say.

And why not, he exclaims, waving the paper back and forth in front of my nose. And that he'd translate and explain it all for us.

No, I say, I don't want it, and I push the contract away. I won't even take hold of it, the very touch, the very feel of such a contract sickens me. And I exclaim: Forcing a child . . .

But he wasn't forced, he says and puts the contract, which I haven't read and haven't even touched, back in his pocket.

What then, I exclaim.

The other thing, he says.

Meaning?

I mean the other word, he says and drags on his cigarette.
The contrary, I mean.

The contrary, I'm thinking. What does he mean? Voluntarily? I ask.

Yes, he says, voluntarily. Seeing that he and his family agreed it had to be so.

Had to be, I exclaim.

Yes, indeed.

And *you,* I say, *you,* I exclaim, were the . . .

Yes, he says and smokes. And he gives his explanation, shuffling up and down between my wife and me, she ashen, me grotesquely festooned, I don't know what color my face is, because I'm no longer looking at it in the window, but we're both, as anyone can imagine, covered in sweat and dirt on the outside, and, no doubt about it, inwardly parched and drained. In short, he shuffles up and down between us and exclaims: Yes, yes! And that he'd hit on the *idea of the spectacle* during a very cold night, of January 13–14 this same year, thus at the moment when it had been scientifically established that in D. and around it there were no historical remains whatever. The ground under our feet, he exclaims, remember?—suddenly it was empty, forever.

Remains, remains, I exclaim and stamp my feet.

Yes, always these excavations, you see, he says and gives himself a shake.

And what are you driving at, I exclaim.

Want, he says.

What want, I ask.

Ours.

Get to the point now, I exclaim.

But that is the point, he says. By January 13, everything in and around D. had been turned inside out and upside down, and sieved through, but there was nothing, nothing, nothing.

Go on, go on, I exclaim.

That meant there could be no more talk of resources to feed D. Stones, look, he says, puffs at his cigarette and walks to the window and points to the familiar open country outside. And now think, he says, yes, I know what you think, I can see what you're thinking, but think now, for instance, let's say, of the fish in the ocean. But they aren't there anymore, because of the way fishing has been done along the coast during the last decades. With dynamite, he exclaims, puffing at his cigarette, shuffling around. And when in addition the factory repeatedly promised by Rome, the factory which was supposed to save them, as the people had been led for decades to believe, was finally not forthcoming, because it couldn't be afforded, then in and around D. new means of survival . . .

Ha, I exclaim, ha, ha.

Well, tourists, he exclaims, with a shrug of his shoulders, è be, what else? But now the following dilemma, he says. No landscape, no remains. But there had to be something to entice tourists into the region, didn't there? And, once they were in the region, then into the village. And once they were in the village, they'd have to be shut inside and entertained. We have to offer them something, so they'll pull the money out of their pockets and put it on our tables and, when the vacation season comes round again, come back perhaps. And naturally what's offered has to be new, extraordinary, and unique. And as you'll recall, sacrifices, not only of animals, he says, with a shrug, have always been common in this region.

What you're saying is absurd, my dear fellow, I exclaim and knock hard on my head with a knuckle.

Yes, of course, you'll now be asking, he says, who put into the world the incredible lie about our being fond of children. On the other hand, the incessant tragedies, not only at the tower but behind closed windows and doors, are of course unknown to you. The ones that occur because of circumstances you can't conceive of.

Listen, I exclaim and walk up to him, for decades I've been visiting the south, which I love, I've even . . .

You don't know the tragedies, he says sharply.

And I've even been in North Africa, I exclaim.

There are circumstances, he exclaims, his dogmatic right-eousness reaching a peak, of which you can have no conception.

All right, I say, if you say so.

Yes, he says, I do say so. Tragedies, he says, and with his free arm he makes a gesture as if drawing aside a curtain— in a theater, tragedies that would long ago have caused a stir in the world, if anything could still cause a stir. Except that until now they'd had no public, which is why these hundreds and thousands of hidden tragedies—all of them ending bloodily—had become entirely superfluous.

Because, he says, throwing his cigarette butt to the floor and stepping on it, they'd gone against the first principle of any theater, the principle that tragedy (or comedy or farce or masque or psychological drama, et cetera) needs to be *seen*. And then, he says, I've lived long enough in other parts of the world, like Frankfurt, to be completely familiar with what the modern public demands, and I know that public much better than it knows itself. There's no point in telling a public: Imagine this or that. This public, *signore,* doesn't imagine anything, it can't imagine anything, because this public, he exclaims, has no imagination. This public, instead of imagining something, wants personally to see, touch, hear, smell everything. This public, he says, and he points to our suitcases, is so demanding, so spoiled, it has already had all the experiences, seen, tried, tasted, smelled everything, it has already been transported, pushed, and carried past everything, *lifted* up on top of everything. And that he, that it, that we, he says, I mean, he says, that the village of D., which for us is, of course, and should remain the center of the world, had to produce for this new public something new of its own, out of itself, something that didn't exist anywhere else, something that had never yet existed, something which, for rarity, even if on a quite different level, might be compared with the capitals at Monreale or with the cathedral of Palermo, and, like them, would have to be taken in with the greatest astonishment. Something, he says, that nobody could easily . . .

Copy, I ask.

Copy, he says, yes, indeed.

All right, I say and wipe the sweat from my forehead. And why have you come here now?

To invite you, he says, to the little one's funeral. You see, he says, reaching for a fresh cigarette, the procession will be coming past here.

16

□ □

□

And in fact at this moment, as I walk up and down that heavy room in terror, to the ceiling of which, as if carved into it, a strip of sunlight sticks, there enters from outside a piping sound, perhaps music, perhaps a *signal*. Immediately I'm standing at the window. And as I push my head out into the morning air, I see the funeral procession, which is what the supervisor has had in mind all this time, already appearing over the horizon and about to cross the *piazza*. And truly it is, as I can see far off, just as spellbinding as he described it yesterday at the foot of the tower, no, even more spellbinding, even more beautiful. For overnight or maybe only toward dawn, as the supervisor was already standing at our door and wanting to make his proposal to us—which, as we now see, amounted to an invitation to Mimiddu Diagonale's funeral, an invitation we shall refuse, yes, we refuse to have anything to do with it, and not only because time is short, but as a matter of principle and because we're outraged—in any case overnight or toward dawn the entire *piazza*, incandescent like a stage and now through a rosy cloud sunlit from above, also the street outside our hotel and all the other streets, have been strewn with flower petals and fresh branches of palm. How changed a street looks, I'm thinking, when it's strewn with flowers. So that the procession, now approaching, moves on and across flowers, mainly roses. Which I can even smell, since my head is sticking out of the window.

Look, Maria, they've scattered flowers. Look, everywhere! Yes, for the procession, the supervisor answers in lieu of my wife who, as ever, isn't saying anything. And that it's an old custom, to cover the earth with flowers and blossoms for someone's last journey. Good that it hasn't died out, he says and joins me at the window.

Yes, I say straightening up to my full height at the window, one doesn't only see them, one smells them.

Did you hear that, *signora,* your husband smells them, the supervisor exclaims, now behind me at the window. So you should do what he says and come to the window too, or you'll regret it.

It's true, perhaps you really should listen to Herr Hans here this time, I say, although he has many opinions I don't share, but the spectacle and the procession are two quite different things. What's the sense of sitting on one's chair and saying *no* to everything? After all, one doesn't get to see a procession like this every day. Come on then, I call from the window and beckon to my wife, while outside, through the petals the funeral procession surges closer.

THE SPECTACLE AT THE TOWER

You know, I think I'm really going crazy now, my wife says quietly, and she turns away from me. Yes, she turns and sits on her chair with her back to me. Which is supposed to mean that she won't come to the window and she'll get along without seeing the procession. And eventually, her face stained with grime and tears, she even stands up and walks, to get away as far as possible from the procession, over to her wall by the door—the wall I'm also now acquainted with—where she positions herself, thin and pallid. Meanwhile the supervisor is looking over my shoulder and his breath is warm on my neck.

So here's the procession. Since it's coming from the direction of the wall through the gap in which—a mistake —I jumped into the village of D., it's coming toward us at an angle. In advance of it, so that it's unsure if he belongs with it, walks a young man, with slow and deathly sad steps, one arm on a hip, to his lips his long shining instrument with a banner hanging from it, the fanfare-blower, who produces, now and then, so as to awaken the village, a few notes the like of which I've certainly never heard before, always the same notes. Now and then he looks back as he walks, to see if the funeral procession is following him, and then he goes on blowing, reassured. And in fact he succeeds: he awakens the village. The windows, the doors, the winding narrow alleys, which yesterday seemed dead, suddenly come to life, full of movement. People, mainly women, are coming out of the *dammusi* and standing on either side of the street, with scarves over their heads or shoulders. Even the balconies of houses I thought were abandoned are coming alive, as I can see, if I lean far enough out of the window. Whole families, the men wearing suspenders, the women with black scarves, have brought chairs out and are sitting, elbows on the rusty railings, with wide-open dark mouths, sleepy but expectant, while others go down on their knees before the fanfare-blower—isn't it ridiculous?—and make the sign of the cross, quite wildly. Others again, also lame and limping people, shuffle toward the procession and join its ranks or at least creep along supported by a neighbor, a little way. So many people! Who'd have thought it? So many people in D. Gradually, as the cicadas start grinding away again, I settle down in my window, which is low and narrow, but as if made to watch from. If only the supervisor weren't so close. Really it's absurd. Any moment now, burly and impetuous as he is—doesn't he realize it himself?—he'll be pushing me to the right and through the windowpane we're both reflected in.

Don't push like that, I exclaim.

But I'm not pushing, he says, and it's as if he's offended and doesn't know that he's pushing, or doesn't want to know.

Yes, yes, you're pushing and it's no use denying it, I exclaim angrily into the mouth odor which he's laying down over my shoulder. Instead of looking over my shoulder you'll soon be pushing me through the windowpane. And then, when he eventually draws back a bit: And if you don't mind, don't breathe so, down my neck, I exclaim.

But what do you mean, the supervisor exclaims, I'm not breathing down your neck.

Yes, yes, I say, you're breathing down my neck.

The procession, then. Which starts with the standard-bearers, all of them broad or artificially broadened, robust, mustached men, whose peevish looks are intended to bestow dignity, leather halters over the chest, in which they support their perpendicular standards. Then, shoulder to shoulder, in wide ranks, all keeping step, either in Sunday suits or in uniforms of the kind worn hereabouts by postmen, the band, drums and brass, which is playing a measured and probably Sicilian march, rattling and tinkling for miles around in the *macchia,* very different from the simple fanfares. And now we only need to turn our numbed heads slightly toward the umbrella pine to see into the open flank of the funeral procession, shimmering and pompous and perversely decked out with festive bunting and wreaths. Next, into the ranks of the sacristans, one holding a silver pot with a silver whisk in it, probably for subsequent use. Or into the more disorderly ranks of those who are carrying candles and garlands. Or into the catafalque, big as a house—how on earth can they carry it?—with figures of saints and penitents, which must weigh tons, sprouting from among the flowers. Wooden figures which, with hands raised in admonition, empty and rigid and wrong, rain blessings down upon our window, or, entirely in white, kneeling, in simulated agony, wringing their hands in misery, surge past us on the shoulders of the people carrying them. Or at the priest who, in his white surplice and black-rimmed glasses, straightens his stole as he walks along, and at any moment now—he's already opening his arms—will burst into song. And of course into the glass-windowed hearse with the white coffin, drawn by four white horses which wear black plumes in clusters on their brows and don't know what they are hauling, first to the church and then to the cemetery. Which, the supervisor whispers in my ear, you already know, so let's go.

Where? I ask and actually expect the man to say now *To the tower.* Instead, he licks his lips and says: To the cemetery, of course.

No, I say, not to the cemetery.

Not to the cemetery, he says astonished.

No, I say and shake my head.

And why not to the cemetery, he asks, stroking his mustache, directly behind my ear.

Impossible, I say.

Yes, he says, but why?

No time, I say.

And why no time, he retorts.

Because, I say, we have to leave for home.

And where's that, he asks.

In the north, I say, a very long way away.

Aha, he says, near Frankfurt.

Yes, I say, in that direction.

All right, he exclaims, but still let's go and see the cemetery.

First let's go, he says, to the funeral.

No, I say, out of the question.

And why out of the question, he asks. You know the cemetery, don't you?

Yes, I say, I know the cemetery, it's behind the café. And then I tell him, don't know why, it's just passing through my head, that yesterday, when he was standing on the ladder, so as to knock on the tower, we very nearly ran away from him, into the cemetery. Yes, I say, we very nearly ran away from you yesterday evening through the cemetery, before the start of the spectacle.

Why, he asks.

Only we didn't have the courage, I say. But I gladly admit to you that, all in all, this cemetery is a beautiful little place.

Yes, he says, putting in the way we know his right hand on his member. A little place, he says, to which we will all go in the end.

Not at all, I exclaim, we'll be leaving soon.

Well, he says, perhaps you'll be leaving soon, or you think you will, while someone like me, you know, simply can't.

Well, I say, even in your case it may take a little time.

That's something, he says, that you can never tell. *He* can suddenly be there.

Who, I ask foolishly.

Him, of course, who else, he says, austerely. And, keeping his right hand between his legs, he extends the thumb and forefinger of his left hand and thrusts them, like two small horns, in the direction of the hearse that is slowly vanishing from sight, slowly reaching the farthest edge of the *piazza.*

Well, I say, the best one is the one that comes without any suffering.

You're talking of the one that comes in sleep, he asks.

Yes, I say, although any is an outrage, you're quite right

215

about that. And since the supervisor falls silent again, I can't help thinking about it again. Poor Mimiddu, I'm thinking. And that with his twelve or thirteen years he hadn't been here for long. He'd scarcely had time to look around, then he'd raised his eyes high over our heads and trained them on a point invisible to us, and then, before we knew it, he'd left us. No, he'd said, stamping his feet a few times, and thrusting resolutely far from him his future as bootblack or herb-gatherer or jobless person or *pistolero,* choosing to jump for us once, rather than dance to us for a lifetime. And now they're walking behind him, his friends, feeling very awkward, festooned with wreaths and crêpe, tearless, with short steps, his friends who didn't jump, now holding their breath, with downcast eyes, and not understanding anything, or not much. And what they have understood, they won't tell me. Then the supervisor, who keeps on forgetting what I keep on telling him and who crowds in on me far too much and breathes too hotly upon me, is all set to whisper in my ear what they're thinking, but I simply push him away and exclaim: Sh! A dead person. And then: Please don't come so close. And then: Quiet, no explanations! And because the people on the street are turning toward us and wanting to look into the room, I draw the curtains, which are dirty. While outside, on the stage, where the slaughtering place is, an old man kneels down, puts his cap beneath his knees and starts to pray, picturesque, reverent. And what now, I'm thinking.
So let's go, the supervisor says, taking his leaden comb from his pocket and drawing it through his hair.

Where to, I ask.

To watch, he says.

Watch what, I ask.

The funeral, he says.

Impossible, I say.

But he won't believe me. He thinks that when I say impossible, it's still possible. And that as long as he keeps on asking and tormenting me, I'll eventually go to the cemetery, the weather is perfect, and the day still before us is one of the longest. All right, he says, let's go.

No, I say.

Why, he asks.

Because, I say, however long a day it is, impossible means impossible. And just as I'm about to leave the window, supposing there'll be nothing more to see outside, and feeling a need for order, so that I'll go over to our suitcases, although they're already neatly stacked and ready to go, the spectators from the natural grandstand appear in small groups outside. Look, I'm thinking, they're even going to attend the funeral! For they're evidently part of the procession and evidently they're going to the cemetery. And over my shoulder I exclaim to my wife, whom I'd almost forgotten in her corner: Maria, look who's coming now! The people from the grandstand. They're going to the funeral. And in fact—isn't it strange—before the procession disappears, they've all—the Englishman with his binoculars, the Japanese with their cameras, the Swiss with his wife—quickly joined it and, some laboriously, sweating already, although it's early in the morning, are

walking along with the procession, just behind Mimiddu.
At all costs they want to be at the funeral.

Look, the supervisor says, resting his bristly chin on the
back of my neck, they're all going to the cemetery. So why
don't you? he says.

No, I say, you're wrong.

And why not, he asks and his lips are suddenly at my ear.

Stop this, I say and push him away.

Then two or three old cars follow behind, with black
ribbons on their antennae; they honk three or four times,
then comes a young man at the same pace riding a Vespa,
finally an old woman with a basket full of fresh pastries,
and that's the end of the procession.

Please let's go and see the funeral, he says and lays his
paw on my shoulder. And now he's really making as if to
drag me, by force, away from the window and through the
empty hotel into the procession at this last moment as it
gradually disappears over the edge of the *piazza*, evaporates,
as it were, in the morning sun, but I simply push his hand
away and say *No!* And turn around in my window and
look him in the eye. When he sees that I'm strong and
determined, he's silent for a moment, but then once again
I say one word too many.

You simply come into our room, I say, at screech of dawn,
drag us out of bed where we are fast asleep, scratching at
our door, and now you're trying to do something without
any purpose whatever. For hours you try to talk us into
seeing something we don't want to see and for many
reasons, too, *cannot* possibly see. Even when for a long

time those reasons, I say, have been no secret to you. That's how it is, isn't it, Maria? I exclaim toward the corner where my wife is, but my wife as usual doesn't answer, she says nothing at all.

You're referring to the event of this morning, aren't you, he asks, the funeral?

Yes, I say, the funeral.

And why don't you want to see the funeral, he asks, the singing will be extremely beautiful.

Because, I say, singing or not—and I'm on the verge of answering, then can't explain why I don't want to see the funeral, and I simply say: No.

But over and over again, don't you notice it, the supervisor shouts, knocking his head with his fist, you're saying the same thing. Over and over again you say *No*.

Because you keep on asking me, I shout, and I knock my head too, over and over again the same question.

Yes, the supervisor says, but I'm only asking if . . .

And the answer is *no,* I exclaim and look out over the *piazza* which, partly sunlit, partly in shadow, is empty again, only the carpet of flowers still lies there as a sign that I hadn't merely imagined the procession—although that would have been of course the best thing. Yes, a carpet of flowers which, however, is now crushed and trampled, as if a great millipede had trundled unrelentingly over it. No, not a pretty sight! Yes, I exclaim in a moment, can't you see that my wife and I are waiting? Can't you see, I exclaim, turning my back on the *piazza, how* we're waiting? If we weren't waiting like this, we wouldn't be standing around like this. Waiting for our car, I exclaim, which must be arriving from the garage at any moment. Ah, if only it would come!

But the funeral, the supervisor says, and he's not even listening to me, has cost a lot of money.

What do you mean, I ask.

I mean the flowers, he says, the candles, the wreaths.

Yes, I say, that costs money. And even then, I'm thinking, it didn't do any good, it hasn't helped the village. Even after we'll have been back home a good while, nothing here will have changed. To the supervisor, who is naturally very disappointed, after all he's been through, and because we're not going to the cemetery, I say: I think that one simply has to reconcile oneself to the fact that things sometimes don't work out. True, one can stand on a ladder and talk a person into doing something, and give him one last push, one can talk a person into doing *anything,* but then for quite various and unforeseeable reasons the thing goes wrong.

Yes, he says, scratching his ear, it has cost a lot of money.

Then suddenly my wife shrieks from her corner: Don't give him any.

What, I say and turn around.

He wants money, she shrieks. Don't give him any.

But I'm not even thinking of it, I say, and I tighten my hold on the wrist-purse. And take a step back from the supervisor, having only now realized that he's begging, and it embarrasses me. But my wife's behavior, too, her shrieking, embarrasses me. And at this moment, as I'm wondering what to do and how to get rid of both of them, one now, the other later, to my indescribable joy and relief I see the *meccanico* really and truly appearing at the opposite edge of the *piazza,* and, on account of the flowers, crossing the *piazza* on tiptoe. Here! Here! I shout to him from my window and I reach up as high as I can and beckon to him. The *meccanico* has no sooner seen me than he quickens his pace and hurries with long leaping strides toward our hotel, toward me. How young, how handsome, how strong he is, as he comes closer! My hand for a long time clasps his, which he reaches out to me through the window, and won't let it go. Saved, I'm thinking. And in fact, once he's arrived, everything happens very fast. I've hardly taken his hand in mine when he tells me that we needn't have any more fears about our onward journey, that our problem, a defect in the transmission disk, as he explains to me in good German, has been solved, at least for the time being, and the car is ready to go, although, because of the *parade* and the many beautiful flowers scattered everywhere here, he hadn't driven it to the hotel, but had parked it by the wall. Parked it, that is, in the same spot from which he'd collected it yesterday, the gap in the wall. And here are your keys and here's the bill, he exclaims. And he even helps me, when I've paid the bill, which seems high, but in view of our circumstances very reasonable, passing the money through the hotel window —I've positioned myself so that neither the *meccanico* nor the supervisor can see into my briefcase—to carry our luggage across the *piazza* and through the gap in the wall, while my wife stays in the room and walks with short but now much sharper and more resolute steps around the remaining suitcases. While the supervisor, who of course hadn't anticipated the sudden appearance of the *meccanico,* stands around looking upset and not knowing what to do, how to behave, what else to explain to us. Should he help me carry the cases or help my wife watch over them? And neither my wife nor I want him and we keep pushing him out of the way, so that after running back and forth between us, grumbling first *in* and then *outside* the hotel and trying in vain to make friends with us, he finally calms down and positions himself, with cap, cane, and legs apart, not far from the pine tree, sighing now and then, or trampling on a rose petal. And he follows our comings and goings with dark distrustful looks out of the corners of his eyes. As for me, after settling vociferously with the cook our hotel account and shaking the hand of the *meccanico* once more and receiving from him, in return, before he leaves, the defective part of our transmission disk, a buckled spring, which I put in my pocket at once, keeping it in that pocket until our return to R., I carry our last suitcase in my left hand and guide my waxen, bloodless wife, who is inwardly and outwardly altogether finished, past the fallen black tree trunks and over the *piazza* for the last time. Once more—the transformation. Once more, the theatrical character of the scene, the sense of being no more than a phantom here, one that will vanish as soon as it has played its brief part. Then, as we're walking away from D., the supervisor, whom we thought we'd got rid of, starts to follow us, hesitantly and at a distance. Yes, we can definitely hear the tapping of his cane. I take a tight hold on my wife's upper arm with my free right hand and say: Now listen very carefully. Don't turn around. Act as if he weren't there. Do you hear, I ask, do you understand? And hope in this way to shake the supervisor off. And in this way, ruthlessly, forcibly I push and pull and drag my wife first across the *piazza* and then, using the gap in the wall and lifting her easily off the ground and through it, out of the village of D. Where to? To our car.

17

Just as we're getting in, I've still got the key in my hand, a final misunderstanding occurs between the supervisor and me, as follows. He has meanwhile caught up with us, he reaches the car just after we do, and he comes puffing and blowing, with overlengthy strides, and excitedly, toward us. And now he tries to tell me something but is too much out of breath. Me, as I move to encounter him, I'm ready for the worst, because of the misunderstanding, and I put my hand in my trouser pocket. But not into the one with the broken spring, to which, as I suddenly realize, we owe our entire dilemma. For obviously all our troubles can be traced back to the breakdown. No, I put my hand in the other pocket, the right-hand one, where the knife is. On Herr Hans I see no weapon, but he has a cane, whereas I, on the other hand, am laboring with the cameras which, in a situation like this, are a great handicap. So that when he suddenly holds the handle of his cane up in front of his teeth, or seems to be doing so, I kick the man suddenly on the shin with all my strength.

A hard kick, yet I'd never have thought this man was so weak, so vulnerable, in his nether parts. How could I have anticipated that he'd at once fall down? So that, when this robust man with eyes closed and limbs outstretched is lying before me in the ferns, I think he's dead and see myself dangerously involved in this death. And the prisons in Sicily, as anyone knows, are not for pleasure. But then he isn't dead, on the contrary he's complaining that he's hurt. Hurt? Yes, I walk closer, relieved, no, delighted, anyway quite unmoved, hardly wrinkling my brows. Where? What a question. His leg of course, the one I kicked. Something broken.

Broken, I ask, moving even closer.

Yes, he says, *kaputt*.

Kaputt, I ask and lean over him.

Yes, he says, probably. Would you be so kind as to help me, he says, stretching far from him the leg I've allegedly injured.

Help him? Again? Still? All right, I'll help. And I call to my poor wife, beckon to her to come back from the car. And stoop over him and ask where it hurts. Where's it supposed to hurt? Until the supervisor lying before us in the ferns, with a crimson face and groaning, actually opens his quasi-waxed trousers—which are, as we guessed, much too tight, and rips them off, exclaiming: Here, it's here! And then we see, my wife and I, shoulder leaning against shoulder, holding one another's hands for safety and stooping low over him, something that had till now escaped us. The supervisor is a cripple, he has a wooden leg! What a *surprise!* We can hardly believe it at first. We put our hands to our heads. Can he really be a cripple? Well, who'd have thought it? Such an able-bodied agile man, so strong and broad, such a ruthless man! On the other hand, it can be no surprise for us. Nothing can surprise us anymore. So that's why he always sweated so much, we're thinking. And at once we know all. Also we knew that he dragged one leg. At once we're thinking of the way he walked, of the ladder and how he climbed it. And also of the crunching, like sand, we're thinking, which always came from his person on our walk to the tower. Yet we'd thought of this crunching as a personality trait, not as something due to his being a cripple. And now this crunching, it turns out, comes from the joint, for his knee, too, is artificial. Our horror on seeing that it's artificial and that the whole left leg is missing! And our abhorrence, as—he has pulled his trousers away—we see the stump itself! And with a grand gesture the supervisor points to this stump. There, says the gesture, a cripple is what I am. As if it were *my* fault, as if I myself had torn his leg off! Like most one-legged men, the supervisor is very soft at the hips, very fat, very white. Much softer and much fatter, of course, than we'd imagined. Because he doesn't get enough exercise, we're thinking. On the other hand he was stepping very lively only yesterday, on our way to the tower, and he walked at a great speed following us to our car. And to this horrible pink, raw, or half-raw stump is strapped, with hooks and straps and buckles, a hand-carved artificial leg, but a leg of high artistic value, made of a light-colored wood, perhaps from a lime tree. Or at least it *was* strapped, for, either because of my kick

226

or because of his fall, the leg has come away and is hanging loose from the stump. Our disgust, on seeing how loose it is! The moment he sees our disgust he tries to explain.

An accident, so long ago I can't even think of it, he exclaims from the ferns. But now that for no reason at all, forgive me for saying so but it's true, you've kicked my leg, it all comes back. A fall from a tall building, he exclaims, which I survived, by a miracle, but down there everything was *kaputt*, of course.

And he starts to tell a new story—words, words!—but I make a dismissive gesture, for we've no wish to hear of yet another fall. Instead, the lower, thus the more fantastic and artificial, if not artistic part of his leg, which, together with the knee joint, has slid away from the stump, has now first to be taken off, because it can't otherwise be strapped back on. And who is going to take the artificial leg off? Well, since it was I who kicked his leg, even if I hadn't meant to, I have to strap his leg back on again. And take it off, too, who else? Amazing, I'm thinking, while I stoop—the cameras hanging down—over the supervisor and untie the straps completely and take off the leg and lean it against the wall, the foot with the shoe on it uppermost. And against this wall, in the morning sun, among the knee-high ferns, the artificial leg will be leaning for quite a time, while I pull at the straps. Meanwhile, out from under the supervisor, a lizard comes, settles beside him, and will sit for a longish time, motionless on a warm stone. Until I take hold of the leg again— speechless, of course, what is there to be said?—and, under the incredulous gaze of my wife, stick it back on the

227

stump, the bit that's left. And connect it to the stump again, using the buckles that are on the straps. Unthinkable how anyone could move with one leg through the village of D., and even to the tower, walking, climbing. It's because I always forget that I haven't got two legs, but only this one here, the supervisor says, and points to his real leg.

What do you mean, I ask.

That I would never have told you, he exclaims, pulling his trousers up again, about my weakness, if you hadn't, I don't know why, kicked me so hard. Of course, I don't feel anything in my shin, the pain is higher up. Forgive me, I say, it was a misunderstanding. I had no idea. If I'd even had the slightest notion, the vaguest suspicion . . .

And you had your cane, I say.

But I need the cane, he exclaims.

What for, I ask.

Walking, he says.

Forgive me, then, I say. I was so *angry* with the supervisor at this moment. Why had he got a leg missing? How I *detested* him! Do I have a leg missing? Does my wife? And while I'm absorbed in his handicap at this moment, I happen to look at his head. What if that were artificial too? Forget it, I'm thinking. When his trousers are buttoned up again, I hand him his cane, but instead of standing up with it, he whacks it against his leg a few times. Against his artificial leg, of course, with the result that the lizard, terrified, vanishes underground again. Is he in pain, desperate, to be whacking himself like that? Well, if only one knew. As with many things that pass through our minds this morning, we don't speak out but just stand there feeling embarrassed and saying nothing, staring at him, and we're fundamentally less concerned with him than, as usual, with our own possessions, in this case the car with its doors open, and with the cameras. You never know what a man's capable of, even when he's lying in the ferns. Eventually, I haul him to his feet—I can hardly leave him lying there—out of the ferns again. For a person who sweats so much he has very cold hands.

Right then, I exclaim, up on your feet, walk! And then, clapping my hands: Move, I exclaim, move!

And since he still doesn't move, but simply stands there, I first quickly dust off his coat and slap the dust off his trousers. Yes, even his cap that had fallen on the ground when he collapsed, I pick it up and give it back to him. A remarkable garment! Yet I shook even his cap out, cleaned it, knocked the dust off it.

There, put it on, I exclaim.

And as he puts it back on his head—impenetrable to me— I ask him how he's feeling.

Feeling, he asks, grabbing hold first of his arm, then of his head, how should I feel? And he limps back and forth a bit in front of me. As I always do, of course, he exclaims, nothing's any different, of course I'm fine.

So we can leave him, put him behind us, with a good conscience. For my wife that's easy. She simply walks away, simply leaves him standing. Maria, I call after her, aren't you going to say good-bye? No, she won't say good-bye, she doesn't even turn around. But me, because I'm the *man,* I've kicked him too and he's a cripple, I give him not only my change and the small Sicilian bank notes which anyway seem suspect to me, but pulling my coin purse from my wrist-purse somewhat laboriously, I give him a not exactly small but also not exactly large bank note. Which he accepts, with arms outspread and making a bow, and which, curiously enough, he kisses. What he does with the note later I don't know, but for now he just gives it a kiss. And now go away, go away, I say, and try, without giving him my hand, but with a slight hiss, to chase him quickly away, through the gap in the wall, up the stone path, and into the village, whose name I don't want to remember, but he insists on our shaking hands. A handshake? Yes, indeed, a handshake. All right, we stand there. And we look at one another once more and extend our hands. God, I'm thinking, as I shake his right hand, what have you taken hold of now? But on his hand, as on mine too, as I ascertain with a furtive glance after the handshake, there's nothing unusual, it's fairly clean, fairly dry, fairly fresh. And I'm thinking that the *rod people,* as well as Maria's pregnancy and Mimiddu's death-act and this wooden leg which Herr Hans has in his trousers, are just things one thinks about for a while, but, once one has reached home, quickly forgets again too.

18

□ □
□

Good, so we're alone again, me and my wife. Not saying
a word, we stand there facing one another. Quickly we
exchange a few lies, utter a few sighs. Embracing one
another, we also kiss. There's to be no more talk about
divorce, we're looking forward to being at home again.
That means looking forward to seeing our eight-year-old
daughter, Adriana, who's living for the time being with
Maria's mother, and is hysterically waiting for us and the
presents we've promised her. Perhaps we shouldn't always
be so preoccupied with ourselves, I say, placing the cameras
in the car. I'm a bit over forty now, well past the halfway
mark in what's called *a human life*. Without noticing it
at all, I've reached this age whose approach used to horrify
me. So that was it, I have to tell myself now, that's what
it has been. With this thought on my mind I've been
sitting more and more often in doctors' offices recently.
In their white waiting rooms I look at their magazines.
But their diagnoses have been, till now, so they assure me,
negative.

You're still healthy, they exclaim and push me out through the door. Professionally, too, I can still expect promotion, even if it's only inside the department. I'm too old for a move up into the central office in B. Well, I won't complain, it's all the same in the end. And then, as I bring my wife to the car door, in the sun, among the trees, in the grass the scraping of cicadas again. Yes, it'll be a beautiful day. A small storm, though, far away in the distance a cloud is forming over the sea. Strange, that the disks of the sun and the moon, so little to choose between them, should so terrify me with their pallor. Yet all fear in that direction is groundless, they don't belong on our earth. Yet not much is left of the once abundant fauna of the region, only the rat, the fox, perhaps the wolf. What folly, always to be preoccupied with ourselves and our relationships, I exclaim, or I think I do, as I quickly get into the car. Suddenly a presentiment of the truth about how the world is arranged, about Maria, Mario, M. Diagonale, about the supervisor, and about me.